Adams

Knock Three Times!

Knock Three Times!

by

MARION ST. JOHN
WEBB

WORDSWORTH CLASSICS

This edition published 1994 by Wordsworth Editions Ltd,
Cumberland House, Crib Street, Ware, Hertfordshire SG12 9ET.

ISBN 1-85326-132-7

Printed and bound in Finland by UPC Oy.

CONTENTS

Knock Three Times!

KNOCK THREE TIMES!

CHAPTER I

Aunt Phœbe sends a Birthday Present

THIS story really begins with the arrival of a brown paper parcel addressed to Molly, but while the postman is bringing it along the road, there may be just time to explain about Jack and Molly's birthday, so that you will understand why Molly sat down to supper wishing earnestly that silver bangles were considered useful and necessary presents.

Jack and Molly were twins, and this was their ninth birthday. Such a happy, exciting day it had been; it *felt* like a birthday all day long, so you can guess how jolly it was, and how special it made Jack and Molly feel. Little did they guess what a weird and mysterious end to the day was now approaching.

They had received a number of beautiful presents, and, to their unbounded joy, a fine new bicycle each from Mother and Father. But there was one particular thing that Molly had wanted for her birthday, and that was a silver bangle.

"Like Mother's," she had told Jack, "only silver. One that nearly slips off when I hang my hand down and that I have to push back up my arm—and it jingles."

As there happened also to be one other thing that Jack wanted specially, a box of paints, the two children had decided some days ago to write to their Aunt Phœbe, who always remembered their birthday, and hint to her as delicately as possible what the most acceptable presents would be. It had been a forlorn hope for Molly, because Aunt Phœbe had fixed ideas about useless and useful presents. Probably she might consider a box of paints useful to encourage Jack's artistic leanings; but a bangle——! Still, Molly sent her letter and hoped for the best.

On looking at Jack and Molly you would have noticed at once that they both had the same kind of brown, curly hair and the same frank expression about the eyes; but while Molly's eyes were brown, and her face often wistful and dreamy, Jack's eyes were blue, and his expression alert and full of energy; there was a certain reckless air about Jack. . . .

A Birthday Present

But the postman has reached their house, and is handing in two brown paper parcels, and so the story really begins.

"It's Aunt Phœbe's handwriting!" Jack exclaimed, as he seized his parcel.

"Yours looks flat—like a paint-box, Jack," said Molly breathlessly, tugging at the string of her parcel.

"Yours looks like something in a box too. Probably it will be a bracelet," Jack said encouragingly, hoping that it would be, for he felt he should be almost as disappointed as Molly if it wasn't.

Jack was the first to vanquish strings and paper, and with a yell of delight he tore the wrapper off his parcel and disclosed a beautiful, shiny black paint-box. For a few moments Mother and Father and Jack were so engrossed in examining and admiring the box that they did not notice that Molly had unwrapped her parcel, until her intense quietness was borne in upon them, and they all three turned round.

Molly stood by the side of the table gazing tearfully at a round, grey-looking thing half buried in a mass of tissue paper.

Knock Three Times!

"What is it, dear?" asked Mother, crossing over to her side.

"It's not——" began Molly, then stopped because of an uncomfortable lump in her throat.

"Let me see," said Mother, and she picked up the grey thing and turned it over in her hands. On the other side was pinned a slip of paper, on which was written:

FOR MOLLY

Hoping she will be a good girl on her birthday and have many happy returns. I thought this useful little thing would do for her dressing-table.

With love from AUNT PHŒBE

"Why, it's a pincushion!" said Mother.

"What a beastly shame!" said Jack.

"Be quiet, Jack. It's a very pretty one," Mother added consolingly.

"Funny shape, isn't it?" queried Father.

"It's—let me see—why, it's the shape of a—what do you call those things?—pumpkins. It's shaped like a pumpkin," answered Mother.

"But it's grey," objected Father. "Why didn't

they make it yellow or green while they were about it?"

"I suppose Aunt Phœbe thought grey would keep clean longer," said Jack: "that's why she chose it."

Had Aunt Phœbe known when she bought 'this useful little thing' what it Really Was—could she have foreseen any of the mysterious happenings that were to follow the arrival of her birthday present —she would have preferred to send her niece half a dozen of the most jingly silver bangles ever made; for she disapproved of adventures in any shape or form, even more than she disapproved of bangles. Yet it was entirely through Aunt Phœbe that Jack and Molly took part in the adventure of the Grey Pumpkin at all.

CHAPTER II

The Adventure Begins

WHEN Molly went up to bed that night she took the pincushion with her and placed it on the dressing-table, and tried her best to think that it looked nice. "It really will be useful," she told herself, and to prove this she picked up a long pin and stuck it into the pumpkin pincushion, though with a little more violence than was necessary. Then she ran across the room and tumbled into bed.

It was a beautiful moonlight night, and the moonbeams streaming into the room made it almost as light as day. Molly lay there snug, drowsily planning out lovely rides that she and Jack would go as soon as they had both learnt how to manage their cycles; the thought of her bicycle sent a warm thrill through her heart and a smile of content hovering about her mouth.

She could hear Jack in the next room moving noisily about; he always made a dreadful noise in

The Adventure Begins

his room, thumping and banging things down and whistling shrilly, until he got into bed. And tonight the extra excitement of having a birthday seemed to make the thumping extra heavy and the whistling extra shrill. Presently the thuds and bumps and whistles ceased abruptly, and she knew that Jack was in bed; and to be in bed and to be asleep were practically the same thing with Jack. No sooner did his head touch the pillow than he was as good as asleep, and no sooner did he open his eyes in the morning than he was out of bed and hunting for his stockings. Sleep did not come so readily to Molly. She would often lie awake for a long time after she had gone to bed, thinking and planning, her brain ticking busily.

Molly was just wondering whether it would be possible for her and Jack to cycle to Brighton and back in a day, and whether Mother would let them go, when all at once she became aware that something was moving in her room; a soft, rolling sound came from the direction of the window.

Molly raised her head and gazed with startled eyes across the moonlit room. She could see something large and round moving softly on the dressing-table. It looked just as if—— Surely her eyes were playing her some trick! She stared across at the dressing-table, frightened, yet fascinated. Then she sat up. No, her eyes had not deceived her.

There, in front of the looking-glass, rocking gently from side to side, was the pumpkin pin-cushion, grown to nearly three times its original size, and growing still larger every second.

Bigger and bigger it grew, until it had grown almost as big round as the front wheel of Molly's bicycle; then it ceased rocking (and growing) and remained still for a few seconds; then, rolling quietly along the dressing-table and over the edge, it fell with a dull thud to the floor. Across to the door it rolled, bumped softly against it, and drew back a few paces. Molly watched as the door swung open, and .the Grey Pumpkin passed out on to the landing.

Molly was filled with amazement. What had happened? What did it mean? She remained quite still, hesitating for a moment. Then she sprang out of bed. Her first fear had vanished, leaving in its place an overwhelming curiosity—

16

and another feeling that she couldn't define—she just felt that she *must* follow the Pumpkin.

Her mind once made up, she felt perfectly calm and collected; even collected enough to slip hastily into some clothes and put on her little blue-and-white frock and her outdoor shoes. Never before in all her short life had Molly dressed so quickly.

Meanwhile the Grey Pumpkin was making its way along the moonlit landing to the top of the stairs. She heard it begin to descend—thud, thud —as she whisked into Jack's room.

"Jack! Jack!" she called in a loud whisper. "Don't be frightened; it's only me—Molly. Hush! Are you awake? Oh, Jack, hush!" as Jack uttered a sound between a loud yawn and a groan. "Get up quickly. It's all right. Only do be quick, quick!"

Jack sat up with a jerk.

"What is it? What's the matter?" he exclaimed.

"Hush! Don't make a sound or you'll spoil everything, p'raps. Put on some clothes, quickly, and come with me. Oh, don't ask questions, Jack, but do be quick, and don't make the slightest noise." And Molly ran back to the landing and listened. Thud, thud, thud, the Pumpkin was rolling steadily and slowly from stair to stair, and, judging by the sound, was already a long way down. "Hurry, Jack," said Molly.

It was easy for Jack to be quick, though not so easy to refrain from asking questions, but to tell him not to make the slightest noise was expecting a little too much of him. However, he only bumped twice against the water-jug and knocked his hairbrush off the dressing-table and fell over a chair before he was ready, and, all things considered, he behaved in a very creditable manner.

Afterward, when thinking things over, Molly was surprised at her own calmness in remembering to tell him about clothes and being quiet; but remember she did, and found herself explaining to her brother as rapidly as possible just what had happened.

"I know it sounds impossible, Jack," she said, "but it's true, and you'll see it yourself in a minute."

The two children sped quickly along the landing and down the first flight of stairs, passing from
18

dark shadows into moonlit patches as they went by landing windows, then back into the shadows again and down another flight, and out into the moonlight once more; so on and on, guided by the dull thud, thud of the Pumpkin on the soft stair-carpet below them.

As they reached the top of the last flight the sound ceased.

"It's reached the bottom," whispered Molly.

Jack shook his head incredulously; he had not seen the Pumpkin yet and could not believe it was the sole cause of the bumping noise he had heard on the stairs. When the noise ceased they hesitated about continuing their descent. It was pitch-black at the bottom of the last flight, and Molly thought it would be so horrible if one of them put their foot on that rolling grey thing in the dark.

As they waited they heard a slight bump—then a streak of light appeared, and they saw the back door swing quietly open. The Pumpkin—and Jack could see plainly that it was a huge pumpkin—rolled ponderously out, and the door began slowly to close again.

"Quick!" gasped Molly; and the two sped down

the last flight, and the next moment were standing breathless outside the back door.

Their garden was long, and backed on to a small wood (which had been the scene of many a picnic during the summer months). A low, broken fence divided the wood from the garden; and it was for this fence that the Pumpkin was heading. It rolled steadily on in a quiet, deliberate way that made it the more uncanny.

Jack and Molly followed — two quaint little figures, moving warily over the grass, with glistening eyes and rapidly beating hearts, half fearful, half curious, and very excited. Jack could scarcely believe his eyes even now, and stared fascinated at the moving grey thing in front of him, as it glided under the broken fence and into the wood beyond. As it gained the woodland path the sound of little twigs and dried leaves crackling as it rolled over them came to the children's ears.

Jack and Molly clambered over the fence, and in doing so Jack lost one of his slippers, but did not miss it in his excitement, and they both ran a few steps along the path to get in sight of the Pumpkin again.

The Adventure Begins

It was not so easy to see in the wood, for the trees met overhead and screened out the moonlight. Here and there a stray beam penetrated, scattering little pools of silver light on the ground; and each time the Pumpkin passed into these pools of light the children hastened their footsteps, but faltered again each time it glided into the gloom, where it was difficult to see and there was nothing save the crackling of the twigs to guide them.

Suddenly Molly caught hold of her brother's arm, and they both stood still. The Pumpkin had stopped in the dim light at the foot of a gigantic old tree with a gnarled and twisted trunk. Watching breathlessly, they saw it knock three times deliberately and heavily against the bark, and then roll back a few paces and wait.

There was a low, creaking sound, and the side of the tree swung outward like a door; and the Pumpkin passed in.

The door began slowly to close again. Jack and Molly looked at each other. What should they do? They both felt it was now or never.

" Now ! " said Jack.

" Quick ! " assented Molly.

Knock Three Times!

Like a flash they reached the door and slipped through—just in time. It closed behind them with a muffled thud, catching the sleeve of Jack's coat as it did so, and they found themselves in complete darkness.

Their curiosity and excitement turned to sudden fear when they heard the door close behind them, and they stood quite still, with their backs pressed hard against the interior of the tree-trunk, not daring to move. A soft, familiar rolling sound could be heard a short way in front of them. It ceased, there was a short silence, then came three distinct knocks, followed by a creaking noise, and another door opened on the other side of the tree. As the light crept into the interior of the tree the children saw to their astonishment that it was not moonlight, but daylight, the subdued light of evening.

A quick glance showed them the hollow interior of the huge tree and the distance they were from the open door. As they caught sight of the ground they both gave a start, for it was composed solely of half a dozen branches stretched across from side to side, and beneath the branches was a big black hole that went down and down and looked as if it had no bottom. They realized that they were standing at the extreme edge of the hole, on a little step of thick, sticky clay. However were they to walk over on one of those thin branches to the door on the other side without missing their footing and falling down into the hole? But even as they caught hold of hands, determined to make a desperate effort to cross while there was light to see, the Grey Pumpkin passed out into the daylight, and the door swung slowly to again, and they were left in darkness once more.

They stood stock still, not daring to move.

"Oh, Jack, whatever shall we do?" said Molly, almost crying.

"Knock on the door behind us and go back home," suggested Jack. "Let's get out of this old dark hole, and the Pumpkin can go where it jolly well likes. . . . Leave go my arm a moment, Molly, and I'll turn round and knock." He turned to suit the action to his words, tearing the corner of his sleeve out of the crack as he did so.

"But, Jack," Molly said hurriedly. "Wait a minute. . . . Somehow . . . I've got a feeling that we *ought* to go on, if only we could. . . . Don't

23

knock yet, Jack. . . . I feel as if somebody wants us, through that door on the other side . . . if only we could get across. Oh, Jack, do be careful—you'll slip!"

"Look here," said Jack, "are you afraid to chance the crossing—do you really think it's worth it?"

"The Pumpkin must have rolled across without the floor giving way—but then, it—he—I mean, what shall we do, Jack?"

"Shall we try?" suggested Jack.

Molly hesitated. Then "Yes, let's," she said. "Only—shall we?" she faltered.

"You stay here while I go across and knock three times on the other door," said Jack, at once decided. "Then while it's light you run across."

"Oh, Jack, do be careful," cried Molly.

For Jack had already started. He felt with his foot for the thickest branch and stepped recklessly forward. To his delight he found that it was quite easy to walk across, and all their fears had been groundless.

"Why, Moll," he called joyfully, "it's as easy as anything. Wait a sec. I'm almost there."

The Adventure Begins

He reached the clay step on the other side and gave three good knocks to relieve his feelings. With a low creaking the door opened slowly, and as the light streamed in Molly ran quickly and easily across, and the next moment they both stood outside the tree, and the door was shut.

CHAPTER III

The Other Side of the Tree

THE two children gazed in astonishment at the unfamiliar scene in front of them, for here was a place they had never seen before, and yet, apparently, a place within ten minutes' walk of their home—a place that led out of the little wood at the end of their garden. And they thought they knew every nook and corner of that wood, and of the fields and lanes beyond for several miles round their house. Yet here was a place they had never seen before; and, more puzzling still, the soft glow of evening and sunset had taken the place of the moonlight and gloom which had been all around them in the wood. For they were still standing close to the same big old tree, but instead of the wood continuing for a quarter of a mile on, and ending at the edge of Farmer Hart's cornfields as it always *had* done, it ended abruptly right in front of them, by the side of a broad white road. This road stretched away to the left, up and

The Other Side of the Tree

up a big hill. You could see it winding like a white ribbon, bordered by the green and brown trees of the woods that clustered on each side. And, at the top of the hill, where the road ended, glistened the white walls and roofs of a distant city. To the right the road continued past the wood where the children were standing, and sloped down, down, till it was lost to sight in the burning crimson and gold afterglow of the sunset.

Jack and Molly looked up the road and down the road, but all was silent, and not a soul in sight. Then a wisp of blue smoke among the trees on the opposite side of the road caught their attention, and they saw that it was curling from the chimney of a snug little red-roofed cottage, which nestled, half hidden, on the fringe of the wood across the road.

The children looked at each other in bewilderment. Then they turned and examined the giant tree behind them, but that did not help them much. It was certainly the same tree, but it was not the same wood. Something queer had happened—it did not seem to be even the same country. They looked up and down the road again, and behind them and before them—and listened. But all was silent. Their eyes wandered back to the curling blue smoke, the only sign of life within sight.

"Better ask some one where we've got to," said Jack, eyeing the smoke.

"But where's IT gone?" began Molly, then broke off quickly. "Hush! What's that!" she said.

She plucked Jack's sleeve and drew him into the shadow of the trees. A distant sound of voices came floating through the still evening air. There were evidently two speakers, for, as the sounds drew nearer the children could hear a high, loud, jolly voice, flowing continuously, and punctuated every now and then by a low, mumbling voice. After a few seconds the words of the high-voiced speaker became distinguishable.

"Stuff and nonsense!" it cried shrilly. "Pull yourself together, Father. Come now, come now, snap your fingers in its face! Laugh at it, I say, and—tss——" The speaker made a little hissing noise. "Where is it?"

The other voice here murmured some reply too low for the children to catch.

The Other Side of the Tree

"What's that?" replied the first speaker. "No —not *you*. But I'll tell you what will happen, you'll be having an attack of melancholia——"

"Oh, not that, not that!" The low voice was raised and pleading. "Don't talk of melons, Glan, don't, I pray you. They make me think of those lemons—and the—and——"

"Now don't you think of that any more," ordered the high voice. "Come, come, come. Pull yourself together. . . ."

The speakers became visible, wending their way through the wood in which the children were standing. One was a young, fat, rosy-cheeked man, with a jolly smile, wearing a white overall and white baker's cap; he was clean-shaven, and was the possessor of the high voice. His companion was a striking contrast to him, being old and thin and pale, with a long white beard; he was dressed in a rich, dark-coloured robe, and had a number of keys dangling from his belt. They pulled up short when they caught sight of Jack and Molly; then advanced slowly, with sidelong glances at each other and low whispers.

Molly stepped forward.

Knock Three Times!

"If you please," she said, very politely, "could you tell us where we are?"

"Could you tell us *who* you are, little lady? —that's more to the point," said the young man pleasantly.

"I'm Molly, and this is my brother Jack," the little girl replied; which did not enlighten the young man very much.

The old man gazed at them with his small, dull eyes, and ran his fingers nervously through his beard.

"We've only just come — through that tree," volunteered Jack, pointing to the giant tree behind them.

"Through the tree!" exclaimed the old man and the young man together.

"Then you are from the Impossible World," added the young man in an excited, high voice.

"We live in England," said Jack with dignity.

"That may be. I don't know England. But if it lies on the other side of that Tree it is in the Impossible World."

"Why do you call it that?" asked Molly.

"Because that's its name in our geography

books. This is the Possible World, and always was
—except——" The young man glanced at the old
man, who turned his head aside.

"Don't speak of that," groaned the old man.

"Cheer up, Father," cried the young man. "Pull
yourself together now. Snap your fingers and—tss
—it is gone, remember." And he beamed encouragingly down at the thin little old man beside him,
who only looked more depressed than ever at his
son's efforts to cheer him up.

"But how is it we've played in this wood—I
mean that wood—ever so many times and never found
our way here before?" inquired Jack.

"Because though you've walked *round* that tree
many times you've never come *through* it before,"
said the young man. "There are two sides to every
tree, just as there are two sides to every question.
When you 'walk round' a question, do you see both
its sides? No. It is only if you go *into* a question
that you see this side and that. Well, then—when
you only walked round that tree it stands to sense
that you couldn't find yourself here. But when
you go into the tree—tss"—he threw out his hand
—"behold! here you are. It's perfectly simple."

31

Knock Three Times!

It certainly sounded sensible and quite simple as the young man explained it, but Jack and Molly still felt rather mystified.

"But *why* do you call ours the Impossible World?" asked Jack.

"Because it's full of impossible things," replied the young man. "Impossible people, impossible ideas, impossible laws, impossible houses, there is so much impossible misery and injustice, and impossible talk, that it's quite impossible for any possible creature to live in it. On the other hand, this land (which is the other side of yours) is the Possible World now; for a time it was Impossible, but we sent——" Here the old man winced. "I'm sorry, Father. But you must let me tell the little lady and her brother where they are. I know. You go and sit down under that tree, and think of buttercups."

"But they're the colour of lemons," whined the old man feebly.

"Not all of them—think of the ones that aren't. There; run along. I shan't be two minutes explaining."

And he patted his father on the shoulder as the old man shuffled across the leaves to the foot of a tree some yards away, where he sat down, and remained shaking his head and looking on the ground, mumbling to himself, while the young man explained the cause of his depression to Jack and Molly.

"It's this way!" he began, after glancing over his shoulder to make sure his Father couldn't hear. "For hundreds of years this has been the Possible World, because it was possible for everyone in it to be happy. But there came a time when an evil influence crept into the land and made it Impossible. It was through this evil Thing that my Father, who was one of the King's Advisers, lost his place at Court. The whole country was under a cloud. Then, Old Nancy—she lives in the cottage yonder"—he pointed to the little red-roofed cottage with the smoke curling from the chimney, on the opposite side of the road—"Old Nancy, she discovered a spell, and she saved us—she banished the evil Thing to the Impossible World and our world became Possible again. Lately, my Father has been afflicted with dreams that he says always come to him before trouble overtakes the country, and he fears by some mishap that the country may become Impossible again."

Knock Three Times!

"What does he dream of?" inquired Molly.

"Lemons," said the young man; "and do what I can I cannot shake him out of the gloom into which he has fallen. . . . It's strange," the young man continued, "but poor old Father seems the only person who did not cheer up when the World became Possible again. It was a nasty shock for him, being banished from Court; and although they've taken him back and given him another post—I suppose he's getting old. And then those dreams——" Glan's face became serious for a moment. "However, they mean nothing, I'm sure. And now you are here you'd like to see our Possible Country, wouldn't you? I'm afraid as you are from the Impossible World you'll have to get a Pass before you can come into the City—but that'll be all right. You must come and have tea with us. I opened a little baker's and pastry-cook's business when Father lost his place at Court, and I still keep it up—fascinating work, making puff pastry and currant buns. I run a special line in gooseberry-jam puffs. I used to do a lovely line in lemon cheese-cakes, but I've had to leave them off since Father's had those dreams. He can't bear to be reminded——" He stopped, a little out of breath.

The Other Side of the Tree

"We'd love to come up to the City; where can we get a Pass?" said Molly.

"But, I say, what about that thing we were following," broke in Jack, suddenly remembering what it was they had followed through the tree; the interest of meeting their new acquaintances had made the children forget for a few minutes. "We'd forgotten, hadn't we, Molly? We were really following a Pumpkin, you know," he said, turning to the young man.

"A what!" and the young man's voice rose to a shriek, and his eyes grew round.

"A Pumpkin," faltered Jack, a little dismayed. "A Grey Pumpkin."

"Father! Father! It's come back," shouted the young man, wheeling round excitedly.

"Come back!" repeated the old man, rising to his feet and stumbling toward them. "Come back! What has come back? Not the—not——"

"The Pumpkin," gasped Glan, his fat, jolly face pale and his hands trembling.

"Oh, my heart and soul," cried the old man, his eyes wild with fear, wringing his hands together. "What did I warn you! What did I warn you!

35

I said those lemons meant trouble. Oh, my heart and soul, what shall we do!"

The father and son stared wildly into each other's eyes for a second.

"What shall we do, Glan? What shall we do?" the old man quavered, shaking from head to foot.

"Where has the Pumpkin gone?" asked Glan, turning to the children.

"We don't know," said Molly, frightened at the distress of the two men. "It came through the tree before us, we followed it, and by the time we got through it had disappeared."

"I must go and spread the alarm. I must go and warn. Oh, my heart and soul!" the old man sobbed, and turning, he stumbled out on to the white road and waddled rapidly up the hill toward the walls of the city, mumbling and chattering and sobbing to himself, the keys at his belt jangling a dismal accompaniment.

"If it's back, then the country will be Impossible again," groaned Glan. "It was through the Grey Pumpkin that it became Impossible before. But just tell me quickly—how did it happen? What do you know about the Pumpkin, and where did you first see it?"

The children explained as quickly as they could, while Glan stood nodding his head and glancing every other second over his shoulder at the receding figure of his father.

"I wondered how you discovered the three knocks on the tree," he muttered. "It can only be done when the moon is full, you know. You didn't know? I thought you might have discovered it accidentally, when you were playing, p'raps. Somebody from the Impossible World did that before—many years ago. Well, go on."

The children finished their story.

"Oh, it's the Pumpkin right enough," said Glan. "Now what can have happened. Old Nancy must have forgotten the usual sunset spell. . . . No, no, she'd never forget . . . she's never forgotten. There must be foul play somewhere. We must go to her at once and see what's happened. Come!"

And followed by the two children he hurriedly crossed the road to the little cottage opposite, and rapped loudly with his knuckles on the door.

CHAPTER IV

Why Old Nancy Slept through the Sunset Hour

THERE was no sound from within the cottage, and the three waited impatiently for a second or two, then Glan rapped again more loudly. The sound of his knuckles against the little brown door rang sharp and clear in the quiet of the evening. They waited. Glan called " Nancy ! " and " Is any one in ? " but as there was still no answer he lifted the latch, and discovered that the door was unbolted. He pushed it open.

They found themselves in an old-fashioned, low-ceilinged room, full of shadows cast by the flickering firelight. The trees outside the house excluded the faint sun-glow, so that the room was dim and nothing could be clearly defined in the farther corners. A quaint red-brick fireplace took up nearly one side of the room, and in a chair by the hearth there sat a huddled-up figure.

Why Old Nancy Slept

"Nancy! Old Nancy!" said Glan, breathlessly, stepping further into the room. "What's the matter, Nancy?"

The figure remained motionless. He bent over it, shaking it gently by the shoulder.

"There's something queer about this. By thunder!" he exclaimed, peering closer. "She . . . No, she's not . . . she's breathing!" He stood back and gazed at the sleeping figure earnestly. "It's not a natural sleep, though. I don't like it at all. If I'm not greatly mistaken the Grey Pumpkin has had something to do with this."

"What shall we do?" said Molly, in an awed whisper.

"If it is any way possible, we *must* wake her somehow. Nancy! Nancy! Wake up!" cried Glan, and he shook her arm again; there was such despair in his voice that the children took courage to move toward the sleeping Nancy to try and help him.

The light from the fire shed a dull red glow over Old Nancy, and looking at her Molly thought she had the sweetest face she had ever seen. Though much wrinkled, her skin was clear and her expression full of kindliness and quiet strength. Her hair

39

was pure white and peeped out from beneath a snowy mob cap.

"Oh, do please wake up," said Molly, laying her hand on Old Nancy's lap.

Old Nancy stirred, turned her head from side to side and gave a great sigh; then she slowly opened her eyes. Her gaze travelled from Molly to Jack, and then on to Glan. She sat up. Then passed her hand across her eyes and stared, dazed, in front of her for a moment. Her glance came back to Molly.

"Who are you?" she said, in a low voice. "And what's the matter?"

It was Glan who answered.

"The sun has set," he said gravely, "and you were asleep."

With a cry Old Nancy started to her feet.

"No, no, Glan; it can't be true!" she exclaimed. "Oh, what have I done! What have I done! It cannot be sunset yet."

She crossed hurriedly to the window and peered through. A glance at the darkening country-side was sufficient. She turned away, and creeping back to her chair sank into it and buried her face in her hands.

40

Why Old Nancy Slept

There was a dead silence in the room. A cinder fell out of the fire on to the red hearth.

"Well, well." Glan cleared his throat and tried to speak cheerfully. "What isn't well must be made well, you know. No good crying over spilt milk, Old Nancy. Come, come, snap your fingers at adversity, you know. We must all put our heads together and see what we can do. What's the best thing to do first?" he smiled bravely, and Jack and Molly took heart and things looked brighter, although they scarcely knew what all the trouble meant.

"Is it back then?" asked Old Nancy, raising her head.

"The Pumpkin?—yes, it's back," said Glan.

"Then there's not a moment to be lost," said Old Nancy firmly, and with an effort she pulled herself together and sat up straight.

"How did it happen—your going to sleep?" inquired Glan.

"I don't know," said Old Nancy, with a puzzled frown. "Never have I missed doing the spell at sunset. I think I must have been . . . drugged. The Pumpkin must still have a few followers in the country—perhaps one of them drugged me—but

Knock Three Times!

I don't know how they did it, they must have chosen the opportunity carefully, so that I fell asleep just before sunset. . . . I remember looking out and seeing the sun about half an hour before sunset time: and then I sat down for a few minutes . . . and I don't remember anything more. When did the Pumpkin come back?"

"About half an hour ago," said Glan.

"He came through the tree," said Jack, "and we followed him."

"You are from the Impossible World, then," murmured Old Nancy, "where I sent the Pumpkin. But now—this will be the Impossible World again soon, I fear, unless——" She looked earnestly into the faces of the two children, then she smiled faintly. "Will you stay and help us," she asked. "Help us to make our world Possible again?"

"We'll stay. Rather!" began Jack.

"Only—only—what about Mother?" Molly interrupted.

"I will tell you the history of the Pumpkin first of all," said Old Nancy; "and then you shall decide whether you will stay and help us, or go home. If you decide to stay I will see that your Mother is not made anxious about you, until your work is finished and you return to her. But, meanwhile, Glan, what are you going to do?"

"Father has already gone to arouse the City," said Glan. "I think I will follow him and see what I can do; then I will come back and see what the little lady and her brother have decided. But before they can do a thing they must hear the Pumpkin's story from you."

So saying he took off his cap with a flourish and opened the door.

"Keep up heart. Laugh at misfortune, remember, and—tss—— We shall win!" he cried, his fat face all a-smile; and he was gone.

"Sit down on the rug," said Old Nancy, "and tell me, first of all, what you know about the Pumpkin, and then I will tell you why it is the Pumpkin is so dreaded in our country, and how he came to be what he is."

So Jack and Molly sat down on the rug, and after relating what they knew of the Pumpkin and how they happened to come across him, they listened while Old Nancy told them the following story, fascinated by her low, sweet voice, and her kind eyes.

43

CHAPTER V

Which Explains who is Inside the Grey Pumpkin

LONG ago," began Old Nancy, gazing dreamily into the fire, "a great King ruled over this country who had an only daughter to whom he was passionately attached. She was a sweet, frail little creature—very delicate. In spite of all the care and attention bestowed upon her, she grew no stronger; indeed, as time passed, she seemed to grow weaker and weaker, until at length it became obvious to all that the Princess was dying. The King was in despair. All that love, money, doctors, and nurses could do for her was done—but all in vain.

"Then, one evening, someone found a shabby old book at the back of a shelf in the Royal Library. To whom it belonged and how it got there no one seemed to know, but anyway, the book proved of priceless value as it contained a remarkable recipe

44

for curing just such an illness as the Princess was suffering from. I need not tell you all about this recipe now: it is sufficient that one of the most important items was—pumpkin juice. Needless to say, the King seized eagerly at any chance to save his daughter's life, and so all the pumpkins available were quickly purchased and the recipe made up, and a dose of this new cure was given to the Princess. From the very first dose there was a marked change for the better, and with perseverance this new remedy gradually worked wonders in the Princess; she grew stronger and stronger and was soon on the road to a complete recovery.

"And then——

"But first you must know that in order to have plenty of pumpkins on hand to complete the cure, the delighted King had a special garden made in which to grow nothing but pumpkins; and he employed a special staff of gardeners to look after this garden. And every day he would go to the garden himself to see how the pumpkins were getting on. One night, a fearful storm swept over the country; and while the thunder growled and the lightning flashed and the wind and rain struggled for mastery—some strange things were taking place down in the pumpkin garden. For when morning broke—there was not a single pumpkin left in the garden : nor in the whole of the country, apparently. But it was not the storm that had destroyed them all. Under cover of the black night and the storm somebody had come and had deliberately cut off the pumpkins, and destroyed them.

" Now this somebody—although he was not discovered for days afterward—was an evil little dwarf man, who imagined that he owed the King a grudge —and sought to punish him this way.

" Nor was this all. When the Princess's nurse went to fetch her medicine—there was none left. All the bottles were smashed to pieces and the precious liquid was spilled all over the floor.

" The King was terribly upset, and sent messengers far and wide, post haste, to try to get some more pumpkins. But they could not get any. And from that time, as each hour passed, the Princess began to decline again. She got steadily worse, and weaker and weaker as days went by. You can imagine what grief it must have been to her father to see her losing her newly-gained health, to see her

Who is in the Grey Pumpkin

cheeks growing pale and thin again—to see her gradually fading away. He made every attempt possible to get hold of a pumpkin—but it seemed as if all the pumpkins in the land had suddenly vanished.

"At length the Princess lay at death's door; the doctors gravely shook their heads at each other; while the King paced ceaselessly up and down the corridor outside her room. He was waiting thus, torn with anxiety and suspense, when a messenger arrived at the palace with a note for the King, which contained the news that a pumpkin had been found! The owner of the pumpkin would give it up to no one but the King himself (the note continued). Would his Majesty kindly walk down into a certain part of the City, and go to a certain house (the address was given), where he would be met by someone who would place the pumpkin in the King's hands. The King, wondering why the person who had the pumpkin did not hasten with it to the palace, nevertheless did not wait to question, but went at once to the house down in the City.

"It was a quaint, stubby little house; and inside he found a little dwarf man. (The King did not

know at the time that this was the person who had
destroyed the pumpkin garden on the night of the
storm.) Anyway, the dwarf began immediately to
pour out some of the grievances that he imagined
he had against the King. And then he discovered
that the King was not to blame at all. There was
some sort of muddle and misunderstanding, and one
of the grievances the King had never even heard
about. When the dwarf realized that he had en-
dangered the Princess's life for no reason, that it
had all been a mistake, and that he had no cause
at all for the spiteful and wicked thing he had done,
he got unreasonably angry (as people often do
when they have wronged someone who hasn't deserved it). And so the dwarf fell to blaming and
cursing the King, and finally tried to make a bargain
with him concerning the pumpkin, which he had
hidden, he said, refusing to disclose its hiding-place
until his demands were granted. The King, whose
sole idea was to get the pumpkin as quickly as
possible, first pleaded, then commanded the dwarf
to fetch the pumpkin immediately: he was willing
to give any price for his daughter's sake. But still
the dwarf haggled and delayed, until the King lost

all patience and a fierce quarrel ensued. In the midst of their quarrel there came the clattering of horses' hoofs on the cobbled road without, and then someone rapped at the door of the dwarf's house. The angry voices within ceased, and in the silence that followed a bell could be heard tolling. And the King learnt that his daughter was dead.

"He returned to the palace, telling the messengers to arrest the dwarf, and place him in the palace dungeon. 'For I shall hold you responsible for my daughter's death,' said the King.

"Afterward, when the whole story of the dwarf's treachery became public, it was discovered that he had not been alone on the night of the storm: others had helped him to destroy the pumpkins: it would have been impossible for him to make such a clean sweep of all the pumpkins in the countryside by himself. It had been a carefully organized plan, of which the dwarf was the ringleader and originator. But none of the others were half so blameworthy as the dwarf; they obeyed his orders without knowing his motives, and did not realize the mischief they were doing was so serious. One or two of them were arrested and received light punishments; some the authorities could not find. But the gravest offender was the dwarf, of course, and for him was reserved the heaviest punishment.

"And this was his punishment. The pumpkin that was found hidden in his garden, the last remaining pumpkin in the country, was brought to the palace, and with the help of a little magic the dwarf was shut up *inside* the pumpkin—where he remains to this day.

"They say that when the dwarf found what his fate was to be, he got very enraged and vowed that if this punishment was carried out, he would make the King and his people rue it, and suffer for it for ever and ever.

"His threat was laughed at, and the punishment duly carried out. About that time a weird old magician happened to pass through the country, and his aid was secured to help with the punishment. He made a spell, and the big yellow pumpkin slowly opened—like a yawn—of its own accord. The little dwarf was lifted, struggling and screaming, and placed in the centre; the magician waved his hands and the pumpkin closed to again. The magician waved his hands again, and a curious grey shade crept over the pumpkin; and it is this grey shade that keeps the dwarf imprisoned. He might force his way out—perhaps even *eat* his way out, who knows—if the pumpkin were still yellow. The grey is part of the magic.

"Well, the King then called a council of Wise Men together, to consider what should be done with the Grey Pumpkin. Some were for keeping it in a museum (and charging a fee of 6d. for visitors to go and look at it); while others advised burying it away in the deepest dungeon of the City, just in case the dwarf ever got out of the Pumpkin; while a third section of the Council, deriding the two former suggestions, urged that the Grey Pumpkin be flung into a ditch beside the High Road, outside the City Gates. The spokesman for this last section was a brilliant, reckless young man, an eloquent speaker; he laughed at the caution which prompted the first two parties to suggest a museum or a dungeon, and looked upon the latter as a grave reflection on the Magician who had so kindly come to their aid. Did they not trust in the spell which kept the Pumpkin tightly closed? he asked the Council. And besides, what person, dwarf, man, woman, or child, would be alive after being shut up in a Pumpkin for twenty-four hours? No, let them show their scorn for the thing by flinging it away, outside the walls of their City.

"Much more than this did the young man say, and in the end he gained his way. The Grey Pumpkin was carried to the gates of the City, escorted by a solemn procession, and thrown into a ditch outside the walls, amid much hissing and booing from the populace. The young Councillor who had suggested all this got carried away by the excitement of the moment, and he dashed forward and gave the Grey Pumpkin that was lying quietly at the bottom of the ditch a good hearty kick: this act was greeted with cheers and shouts of approval from the crowd, until they saw that the Pumpkin, which had been sent spinning, had landed on the High Road, a dozen yards away, and was slowly rolling down the hill. The crowd fell silent, and watched. On, on the Grey Pumpkin rolled, down the hill from the City, past my cottage door—I remember—on, on, until it disappeared at length into a dark forest right down at the bottom of the High Road.

52

Who is in the Grey Pumpkin

"And after that, all our troubles began. The dwarf kept his vow, and made us suffer. Somewhere, down in that dark forest, he got hold of some black magic—no one knows how, or who helped him. All we know is that since that time he has become possessed of certain magic powers, and that one misfortune after another has overtaken our country—all caused by the Pumpkin. Wherever he goes he makes misery and mischief: I cannot tell you all the horrible things he has done, he and his little band of followers—those faithful few who helped him in the beginning to destroy the pumpkins, you remember. They went right over to his side after they were punished, and he seemed to gain some evil influence over them. There are not many of them, but they are in all parts of the country, ready to help him when he needs them. And with his knowledge of magic he could so disguise them that we could not recognize them. But they are powerless without him, and when after suffering him for a long time (because we could not find a way to escape him) we finally discovered a way of banishing the Grey Pumpkin out of our World into your World where he could do no harm,

53

his followers became practically harmless, until to-day.

"That is the story of how the Grey Pumpkin came to be what he is. The King, whom he hated, has been dead many years and another King reigns in his stead. And the young Councillor, the eloquent young Councillor who advised the people so unwisely, was banished from Court; he has grown old and timid and querulous, and is a disappointed man whose career was blighted at the outset through the Pumpkin. You have seen this once reckless, dashing young man; you met him just now in the wood. He is Glan's father."

CHAPTER VI

The Black Leaf

W HAT dreadful things the Pumpkin must do," said Molly, "to make every one so frightened of him."

"He does do dreadful things," said old Nancy.

"What a mean revenge—on innocent people," Jack commented.

"And the worst part of it is," Old Nancy continued, "that no one knows how much evil power he has, nor what he can do to them if he likes. He evidently has his limits, for there seem to be some things that he cannot do: for instance, he cannot roll along quickly—he always moves at the same slow pace; and he cannot climb up walls or trees, though he can roll up hills. So as long as you keep out of his reach he cannot hurt you."

"If he never comes out of the Pumpkin—the little Dwarf—what does he do when he catches any one?" inquired Molly.

"Just rolls up to them and touches them—bumps

55

against them softly—and then—something queer happens to them. Perhaps they are changed into some strange animal, or maybe they shrink until they are only a few inches high, or suddenly they find they have lost their nose or their eyesight—or worse things than these may happen. The misery caused by the Pumpkin is unthinkable; and more often than not—incurable."

"Oh," shuddered Molly. "Well, however did you manage to get rid of him?—to send him into our World?"

"I was just going to tell you about that," said Old Nancy. There was a moment's pause, then, "I am a kind of magician, you know," she went on. The children glanced quickly up at her, startled at her words, but her gentle face reassured them as she smiled kindly down. "And being a kind of magician I discovered a spell that would send the Pumpkin out of our country into the Impossible World. So I turned him into a pincushion, a grey pincushion, and transported him into your World, where I thought he could do no harm; and you know what happened there. I believed we were rid of him for ever, and we would have been—but for me. It was part of the spell that every evening at sunset I should stand with my face turned to the sinking sun, and, making a certain sign with my arms outstretched, should repeat some magic words. As long as I did this each evening the Pumpkin could not come back, and our country was safe. But I knew that if I chanced to be a minute after sunset any evening the spell which bound the Pumpkin would break, and he would return to us." A sorrowful look came over Old Nancy's face. "And to-night," she said, "I failed to say the magic words at sunset—and he has come back. I am certain it is one of the Pumpkin's followers who has foiled me; though how—I do not know."

"Can't you use the spell and turn him into a pincushion again?" asked Jack.

"No," said Old Nancy, shaking her head. "That spell could only be used once, and once only; and I know no others."

"Then however can we——" began Jack.

"Patience," said Old Nancy. "There is one way of thwarting the Pumpkin which everybody in our country knows of. But they can't do it, because they can't find the Black Leaf. . . . You must know that when the little dwarf was thrust into the Pumpkin, the plant in the dwarf's garden on which the Pumpkin had grown, immediately turned black. For thirteen days it remained so, bearing one solitary giant leaf — then, all at once it vanished! And now, each year it comes up in a different part of the country—just this one immense Black Leaf—and it remains for thirteen days, and then it disappears again. We have not looked for it these last few years—there has been no need: still, some people have seen it. But now we want it badly. For if you can find the Black Leaf, and pluck it, you have but to turn your face to the West and say some words (which I can tell you) and wherever the Pumpkin is he will be compelled to come to you: then you must touch him with the Leaf and—you have him in your power. We were in despair before, when no one could find the Black Leaf, until I discovered that spell. And now, as I know no other spell we shall be in despair till someone does find the Black Leaf. And that is what I want you both to stay and help us do. Strangers are often lucky."

"Oh, we *must* stay and help," cried Jack, impulsively, "mustn't we, Molly?"

The Black Leaf

"I should love to," said Molly, "but couldn't we just let Mother know so that she wouldn't be anxious?"

"If you decide to stay," said Old Nancy, "I will take care that your Mother is not worried in any way by your absence. I will send a message to her."

"Then we'll stay," decided both children at once.

"I am so glad," Old Nancy said simply. "And now, if either of you should be lucky enough to find the Black Leaf remember what to do. Pluck it immediately, and stand with your face toward the West, and say: 'Come to me, Grey Pumpkin! I command you by the Black Leaf!' . . . You can remember that?"

Jack and Molly repeated it to make sure, and then Old Nancy went on,

"When the Pumpkin appears—as he must appear —rolling toward you, touch him with the Leaf, quickly, before he can touch you. Then he cannot harm you, but will be compelled to follow you wherever you lead him."

"And where should we lead him?" asked Molly.

"Bring him to me," said Old Nancy grimly.

"There was something I wanted to ask you," said

Jack, "and I can't think what it was now. . . . Oh, I know. . . . Does the Pumpkin know where the Black Leaf is?"

"We are not quite sure about that, but even if he does, it is evidently of no use to him; I mean, he dare not *touch* it—that would be fatal to him. But he can guard it, if he knows where it is, and try to prevent you getting it: and this is what he will try to do whether he knows where it is or not; he is sure to try to delay you or trap you, as soon as he discovers that you are searching for the Leaf. And he will soon know what you are trying to do—one of his followers will tell him, you may be sure. So, beware of the Pumpkin and his little band of people. You are in less danger of being caught by the Pumpkin than you are by one of his band, because you will know the Pumpkin when you see him, but you won't know which are his decoys, his spies, and which are not. And I can't help you about this, you must simply be very, very careful, and do not trust anyone until you are sure. Of course, people like Glan and his father, or anyone inside the City, are quite all right — because nobody will be allowed within the City Gates now without a pass; and they cannot get a pass, if they are one of the Pumpkin's people."

"Mightn't one of the Pumpkin's people find the Leaf?" inquired Jack.

"They dare not touch it either, even if they do know where it is," replied Old Nancy. "But they can guard it—as the Pumpkin can."

"If the Black Leaf only appears for thirteen days each year, how do you know which thirteen days they are?" asked Molly, thoughtfully.

"Because the thirteen days start on the anniversary of the day on which the little dwarf was put inside the Pumpkin," said Old Nancy. "And, as fate decrees, it was the anniversary yesterday, *so the Black Leaf is somewhere above ground now.* . . . Oh, I do hope and trust you will be successful, my dears." Old Nancy clasped her hands together nervously. "And don't be ashamed to *run* if the Pumpkin tries to catch you before the Leaf is found. You are powerless against him and his magic—until you have the Leaf. But he can only use his magic and hurt you if he touches you, remember. So don't let him touch you!"

"We'll *run* all right, if we see him coming,"

said Jack. "Or else we'll climb up a tree or something."

"Well, that's a good idea, too," said Old Nancy.

"I suppose it's really a rather—dangerous sort of work we're going to do," said Molly.

"It is dangerous, and very brave of you to attempt it," Old Nancy said. "It needs courage and perseverance. I think you both have pluck, and you both have perseverance; somehow I think one—but only *one* of you will be successful."

"Which one?" cried Jack and Molly eagerly.

"Ah!" Old Nancy replied, and shook her head mysteriously. "I cannot tell you any more than that. . . . But now we must get to work immediately. There is no time to be lost. Wait here for a moment."

She rose, and smiling at the children, made her way across the firelit room and passed out through a doorway at the far end of the room.

Jack and Molly sat still and gazed silently round the shadowy room. They could never afterward describe the feeling that came over them, alone in that room—even to themselves. They were not afraid. A curious feeling crept over them, and they

The Black Leaf

both felt sure that there was something or someone in the room with them, although they felt equally sure there was no one. There was an air of mystery and secrecy in the room. No shadows danced on walls quite in the way that they danced in Old Nancy's room; no smoke curled in such weird and fantastic shapes as the smoke that curled up the wide chimney in front of them; while it almost seemed ridiculous to say that the chairs were empty when the *something* in the room crowded into each of them.

"'I am a kind of magician, you know,'" repeated Molly softly, nodding her head at Jack. "Do you know I can *feel* that she is."

"So can I," whispered Jack, hoarsely. The children looked at each other seriously for a few seconds, then they turned their heads, and saw that Old Nancy was standing in the doorway watching them. She came forward into the firelight, and they saw that she carried two small satchels in her hands. They were something like the children's school satchels, only they were smaller and stronger in appearance, being made of soft black leather; they had long straps attached to them, to pass over the shoulders.

Knock Three Times!

"These are your knapsacks," said Old Nancy, smiling. "You will find them useful on your journey. This is yours," she said to Molly, "and this is yours," to Jack. "Now if you will open them and take out what is inside, I will explain what they are meant for."

The children thanked her and eagerly unbuckled their satchels and felt inside. The contents of each were the same: a sealed envelope, a box of matches, and a little packet of square, brown things that looked like caramels.

"Inside the envelopes are your Passes into the City. Give them up at the City Gates. Take care of them, without them they would not let you in. The matches in those two boxes are not quite ordinary matches—though they look like ordinary ones. I think they'll help you over one or two difficulties. Use them carefully as there are not many matches in each box. Whatever you do don't light them in the daytime, but light them when you are in the dark and want to see."

"Do we strike them just in the ordinary way?" asked Molly.

"Just in the ordinary way," said old Nancy.

The Black Leaf

" And the little brown squares in the packets are for
you to eat, should you be very hungry, and unable
to obtain food. You will find them wonderfully refreshing—it is something I make specially. . . . And
here," she continued, turning to Jack, and holding
something out to him, " is another shoe for you. I
see you have only got one on."

"Why, so I have," cried Jack, noticing for the first
time that one of his slippers was missing. " Now
wherever did I lose that, I wonder!" (Poor little
slipper, it takes no part in these adventures, as it
is left behind in the Impossible World. It is lying
by the fence at the bottom of the children's garden,
you remember.) "I never noticed it before. Thanks
awfully, though. This slipper fits splendidly. How
did you know my size?"

"Oh, I knew," Old Nancy laughed, and would say
no more.

She helped the children buckle on their satchels,
telling them that once they were inside the City they
would learn what plans were being made for the
search. "I wish I could give you some magic charm
to defend you against the Pumpkin," she said. "But
that is impossible. The Black Leaf is the only thing

that can harm him, and save us all. Be very careful, dear children. . . . Ah!" she broke off with a sharp exclamation.

"What is it? What's the matter?" cried Jack and Molly, as Old Nancy stood gazing at her left hand which she held out in front of her.

"So that's how it was done," she cried. "Look! Look!" and she held her hand toward them. A dark grey mark stained the middle finger from base to tip.

"What is it?" Molly repeated.

"The stain," whispered Old Nancy excitedly, "do you see? It's grey! The Grey Pumpkin's mark! It *was* one of his spies then, who made me sleep through the sunset hour. But why to-day should they have been able to do this, when they have been powerless for so long?"· she muttered to herself. "Could anything have happened to the Pumpkin in—in your world, that enabled him to exert his evil magic all the way into our world, and so the spies were able to begin their black magic again? Can you think of anything that happened?" she asked Molly eagerly.

Molly tried hard to think of something. "Of

course, as it was a pincushion—I stuck a pin in it," she said presently.

Old Nancy gazed at her strangely. "In the moonlight?" she asked. "Was the moonlight shining on it when you stuck the pin in?"

"Yes," said Molly, nervously. "Oh, did that do it? Oh, I am so dreadfully sorry—then it is all my fault that the Pumpkin has returned?"

"No, no," said Old Nancy, "you are not to blame. How were you to know? It was my fault for not being more careful, then they could not have drugged me." She crossed quickly to the window. "Yes—see—here—here on the sill. There's a trace of grey powder. I know what has happened. When I went out of this room earlier in the evening—I did for a few minutes, I remember—yes, just before sunset time—someone must have opened the window and scattered the powder on the sill, hoping that I should go to the window at sunset and that I should put my hand on the sill and touch the powder. And I did. And the powder must have been magic and made me go to sleep. I wonder I never noticed it. . . . But never mind now, never mind now. . . . It is too late. We must get to work at once to remedy the evil."

Knock Three Times!

But Molly still had a feeling that it was partly her fault and she was glad that she and Jack had decided to stay. She felt it was the least they could do—to try to find the Black Leaf.

As Glan had not returned they decided to start out, for the hour was getting late, and Old Nancy thought it would be wiser for them to be inside the City as soon as possible. She told them that they were almost sure to meet Glan on the hill—he had evidently been delayed—they couldn't miss him.

" Good-bye, dears, good-bye," said Old Nancy. " My thoughts will be constantly with you till we meet again. Good luck go with you both."

Leaving Old Nancy standing in the doorway, with the firelight glowing warmly in the room behind her, the two children started out in the dusk and began to ascend the hill.

CHAPTER VII

Glan Opens the Gate in the Nick of Time

THE children walked briskly, glancing from the City lights to the dark woods on either side of the road. Everything lay quiet and peaceful, and overhead the moon was now visible. It seemed impossible to believe that a cloud of fear hung over the City ahead. As they drew nearer the top of the hill the sound of a bell tolling came floating down to their ears.

"What's that for, I wonder," said Molly.

"P'r'aps it's a sort of warning," suggested Jack, "to tell people the Pumpkin's back again."

Molly shivered. "Let's hurry a bit more, shall we?" she said. "I'll be glad when we're inside the City, won't you, Jack?"

So they quickened their footsteps.

"I do hope we meet Glan," Molly went on. "We couldn't very well miss him, though, could we? . . . . You're sure you've got your Pass safely!"

"Rather," said Jack. "At least I think I put it back in my satchel." And diving his hand in to make sure, he jerked the envelope which contained the Pass out on to the road. A passing breeze caught it and turned it over and over on the ground, and there was a hurried scramble on Jack's part to get it back again. He had just put it safely back in his satchel, when a sudden cry from Molly made him wheel round to see what was the matter.

Molly was standing gazing down the hill. "Oh, Jack! Jack! Look!" she cried, pointing to the dark wood on their left. About thirty yards away down the hill, something was slowly emerging from the black shadows of the trees.

It was the Grey Pumpkin.

It rolled leisurely out into the moonlit road, paused for a moment, then turned and moved up the hill toward them.

"Don't be ashamed to run," Old Nancy had said. And they were not ashamed. Jack and Molly took to their heels and ran. They did not want to be stopped by the Pumpkin at the very beginning of

their quest, knowing how powerless they were until
the Black Leaf was found. So they ran with all
their might, on, on, until the City Gate was but a
little farther ahead of them, and the tolling bell
clanged loudly from within.

" Jack, oh, Jack—I—can't—run—any—more,"
gasped poor Molly. "Oh—what—what shall—we
—do?"

"We're just there—keep—up—old girl—only a—
little—bit more—we're—just—there," panted Jack.

With a final effort they rushed forward and reached
the gate at last. Jack flung himself against it and
started beating on it with his fists, and then snatching
up a large stone from the road he hammered it with
that; while Molly seized the thick bell chain at the
side and began pulling it vigorously.

It was a curious gate—more like a door than a
gate—made of solid iron; and at the top, high
above the children's heads, was a tiny grating
through which the citizens could see who stood
without.

Jack glanced despairingly up at the high white
walls and the black iron gate, while he continued
to beat wildly with the stone and shout as loudly as

he could for help. There seemed no way of escape if they did not open the gate, and looking back he saw the Pumpkin coming silently onward.

"It's no good making a dash for the woods, Molly," he exclaimed, " he'd cut us off. Pull harder, and shout too."

So Molly pulled harder at the bell chain and cried out for someone to come and open the gate and let them in.

Suddenly, above the noise they were making and the sound of the tolling bell within, the children heard voices, and a clattering on the other side of the gate. Then a face appeared at the grating.

"Open the gate!" cried Jack. "Quick! Quick! We've got a pass. Open the gate and save us!"

A loud murmuring arose within, and they heard the jangling of keys. When all at once a voice shrieked, "Look! Look! On the hill. It's the Pumpkin! Don't open the gate! Don't open the gate, it's a decoy!"

"It's not, it's not," cried Jack. "Oh, save us, save us. We *have* got a pass. Let us in and save us from the Pumpkin. For pity's sake open the gate!"

Glan Opens the Gate

The voices inside were now loud and angry; the people were evidently not inclined to believe him.

"Oh, Jack, Jack!" screamed Molly. "He's just behind us, Jack!"

Jack wheeled round and saw to his horror that the Pumpkin was near the top of the hill and close upon them. He was desperate. Raising the stone above his head, he flung it with all his strength at the big, grey, moving thing. There was a dull thud as the stone struck the Pumpkin and sent it back a few paces; but it quickly came to a standstill, and began at once to cover the ground it had lost.

Meanwhile a fresh arrival had come upon the scene behind the gate. In the midst of all the hubbub, the angry voices, the clanging bell, the pattering feet, there was a moment's lull, and Jack and Molly could distantly hear the sound of running feet. Then a familiar voice exclaimed : "Hi, there! What's all the fuss about?"

A score of voices started to explain.

Molly gave a sob of relief, "Oh, it's Glan!" she cried.

"Glan! Glan!" the children called imploringly. "Open the gate quick and save us. Oh, *do* be quick!"

Knock Three Times!

Glan's face appeared at the grating.

"Bless my soul!" he cried in his big voice. "Here, give me the keys! Yes, I know it's the Pumpkin too, but if we don't open the gate this instant the little lady outside and her brother will be . . . Give me the keys . . . give me the keys! Decoys? . . . Bah!"

There was a jangling of keys again, the sound of a lock being turned, and the huge gate swung back.

Jack and Molly dashed in, and Glan slammed the gate behind them—just in time. Another minute and the Pumpkin would have got through.

"But can't he open the gate if he just touches it?" cried Jack, tugging Glan's sleeve excitedly.

"No, no, he can't do that!" Glan said, shaking his head as he stood on tiptoe to bolt and padlock the gate securely. "Thank goodness there are some limits to his magic!"

Jack and Molly found themselves in the centre of an excited crowd of people who regarded them curiously, but without anger or fear, since Glan had befriended them. Most of them were chattering and waving their hands toward the gate, but some watched the children with narrowed eyes and then

74

Glan Opens the Gate

whispered behind their hands to their neighbours, while others stood and gazed gloomily at them in silence. They were a picturesque race of people, these citizens of the Possible World, clothed in a bewildering variety of dresses, of no particular style; apparently each person dressed in whichever style took his or her fancy, or which was best suited to the occupation carried on by that person. And this, after all, is the only sensible way to dress. The result of these numerous styles and colours was very pleasing to the eye : at least, so thought Jack and Molly as they gazed round at the animated scene before them.

"Don't you fret," said a kindly-looking woman dressed in dark blue with a blue cap on her head and a chain of dull yellow beads round her neck. "We took care to have the gate washed with a magic lotion, and the Pumpkin cannot touch it—nor the gate at the other end of the City—though we have to keep both safely locked in case a friend of the Pumpkin's were to get in and open the gate for him." She looked straight into the eyes of first Jack and then Molly—and then she smiled.

75

Knock Three Times!

By this time Glan had finished locking up the gate, and was handing the keys back to the gate-keeper—a large, pompous-looking gentleman with a brown beard, dressed in a green Robin Hood style of suit—who seemed inclined to be sulky.

"I'm sorry I could not wait for your permission to open the gate," they heard Glan say. "The matter was urgent, you see. It was the little lady and her brother who are going to try and help us."

"You'd no right to snatch the keys out of my hand like you did," replied the gate-keeper sullenly. "You might have got me into no end of trouble, if they *had* been decoys. Where's their pass, any-way?"

Glan beckoned to Jack and Molly.

"If you wouldn't mind giving up your passes to this gentleman," he said. "Ah, that's right," as Jack and Molly handed their envelopes to the gate-keeper, who proceeded to open them and examine the contents carefully.

Then he slowly nodded his head. "All right this time," he said. "But you be careful in future, young man"; he looked at Glan. "It might have been a very serious matter."

Glan Opens the Gate

Glan's eyes began to twinkle.

"I will certainly profit by your advice," he said. "I'm extremely sorry I had to snatch the keys, I apologize most humbly, but, of course, you didn't understand who it was outside, and what danger they were in . . . and anyway, all's well now, isn't it, sir?"

"Oh, it's all right this time, as I said before."

"Thanks," said Glan. "Well, good-night. . . . And now," he turned to the two children, "you must be very, very tired after all that. Will you come along with me to my little place? Father and Aunt Janet will be very pleased to welcome you."

Jack and Molly assented willingly, and followed Glan closely as he made his way through the crowd. When they reached the outskirts of the knot of people Molly began to thank Glan for coming to their aid at the gate; but he wouldn't hear of it.

"What else could I do, on my life, little lady?" he said. "I have faith in you both, and the help you are going to give us. I want you to come and have a good rest now, and then in the morning you will be told what part of the country to search, and you can start out at once on your adventures."

Knock Three Times!

"It seems as if we have already started," observed Jack. "It seems as if it's been all adventures to-day."

"I think you're right," said Glan. "But there's more to come—though we'll talk about those to-morrow. You must be too tired to-night. I am very glad you got here all right, I was delayed in coming to meet you—I felt sure, somehow, that you'd decide to stay, after you had heard Old Nancy's story. And anyway, I should have been half-way down the hill to meet you, only so many people stopped me to know if the bad news was true—that the Pumpkin had returned—and there were such a lot of things to see to, and I had to run home to tell Aunt Janet to get things ready for you—in case you came back with me, so that I reached the gate just in time to let you in." He stopped a little out of breath.

They had been walking fairly quickly all this time, and the children could now see more clearly what a beautiful City they had entered. Everything glistened, a pure white, in the moonlight. Houses, walls, roofs, chimneys, front doors, gates, pavements, roads—all were white and spotlessly clean. Yet the curious part of it all was, that it was not monotonous to the eye; instead, it seemed to make a fine background for the coloured flowers and trees and dresses of the people. And to-night, the City was full of soft shadows, cast by the objects that stood in the light of the moon. Glan and the two children turned into a narrow, hilly street, down the centre of which ran a sparkling brooklet, that babbled and gurgled as it splashed over its pebbly bed. Most of the houses in this street were quaintly built, with the top part bulging out over the street. And Molly noticed as they passed that all the windows had coloured curtains —in one house all the curtains were blue, in another a deep amber shade, in another a glowing crimson, and so on—which had a very pretty effect, especially if the windows were lit from within. The white houses, the coloured curtains, and the window-boxes full of flowers that adorned each window in the street made a great impression on the children. They thought it all charming, and said so to Glan.

"The Possible World," he said, then shook his head and held up his finger. The tolling of the bell floated across to them.

"I suppose that's to warn people, isn't it?" said Jack.

Glan nodded. "But we'll soon change its tune, won't we?" he said. "It's joy-bells that'll be ringing next, because the Black Leaf is found. And who will have found it. . . . Ah, ha!" he winked knowingly, and wagged a fat forefinger at the two children. "What a great day it will be," he chuckled. "You'll have to be careful I don't win, because I'm going to search too, you know . . . but we'll talk all about that in the morning."

At the top of the hilly street they crossed an open square with a market cross in the centre, and entered another narrow street with bulging houses and shops in it. They met few people now as they continued on their way: many were still down by the West Gate, and others had wended their ways homeward after assuring themselves that the Pumpkin was safely outside the City walls. About half-way up the street Glan came to a halt outside a small shuttered shop, that lay back underneath the frowning brow of the bulging upper story of the building, like a dark deep-set eye. Producing a key from the pocket of his white jacket, Glan placed it in the lock of the side door and opened it quietly.

"I'll go in first, shall I?" he said. "There's no

light in the passage, and you might fall over something."

Jack and Molly followed him into the house, and stood hesitating on the mat while he strode down the passage and opened a door at the farther end. A dim light crept out and thinned the darkness. From the room came a low murmur in familiar tones.

"Come along," called Glan. "Would you mind just shutting the front door. Thanks very much."

It was a small room at the end of the passage with a round table in the centre of it on which stood a shaded lamp. At the table sat Glan's father with his elbows resting on a large open book in front of him, while his hands, held to the sides of his head, covered his ears; an expression of profound melancholy was on his face as he gazed at the children on their entrance. Bending over the fireplace was a genial, comfortable-looking, elderly woman, who was stirring something in a saucepan.

"Bless their hearts, how tired they look," she exclaimed, as she caught sight of the children's faces.

"It's the little lady and her brother that I told

81

you about, Aunt Janet," said Glan. "Is everything ready for them?"

"Yes, my dear," replied Aunt Janet. "The beds is sweet and aired, and there's a bowl of hot broth for both of them, bless their innocent souls, which'll be cooked in a minute or two. Sit you down, dearies, and rest yourselves, and Aunt Janet'll have things ready in no time for you."

"They're sure to be tired," said Glan. "They were chased up the hill by the Pumpkin," he added in a lower voice.

But his father had heard. "What was that?" he asked mournfully, taking his hands down from his ears.

So Glan had to explain to him the incident at the gate, and how the Pumpkin nearly got in. The old man listened intently, groaning every time Glan paused for breath, and rolling his eyes whenever the Pumpkin was mentioned by name. At the end of the story he hastily stopped his ears again, and bent over his book muttering faintly that he "couldn't abide that bell ringing."

"Poor old father," said Glan, compassionately, "it does upset him so."

Glan Opens the Gate

Jack and Molly were glad of the hot broth, and Aunt Janet, as she fussed about them anxiously, was pleased to see that the steaming bowls were soon emptied.

"Sleep well, for there is hard work before you; but courage—and everything will be well," said Glan, beaming down at them as he wished them good-night. While his father shook his head mournfully, and sighed as he gave them each a limp hand.

Aunt Janet lit two long candles, and conducted them up a flight of high narrow stairs to the top of the house where there were two small rooms with little white beds, and freshly laundered window curtains.

"Good-night, dearies," she said. "Blow the candles out safely. I hope you'll find everything you want here." Her eyes grew very kind. "I had a little girl and boy once," she said, "and I know they'd like you to use their things—if they knew—so I've put them all out for you. They were just about your age, and I—and they—good-night, dearies," she stooped suddenly and kissed them each on the forehead.

CHAPTER VIII

Aunt Janet Puts on her Best Bonnet

A SUNBEAM creeping through the window and along the floor to Molly's pillow awoke her in the morning; she sat up with a start, puzzled for a moment at the unfamiliar surroundings; then she remembered—and giving a long sigh, snuggled down again for a few more minutes while she thought things over.

How strange it all seemed, just like some wonderful dream, she thought—and yet it was not a dream. Here were she and Jack in the middle of a real, exciting adventure. An adventure in which they were taking an important, and (she hoped) useful part. What would be the result of their search for the Black Leaf? Would either of them find it? And what had Old Nancy meant by saying that she thought only *one* of them would be successful? Wouldn't she and Jack be allowed to search together, Molly wondered. She hoped Jack wouldn't be sent to one part of the country, and she to another. She

84

tried to recall all the information and warnings that had been given to them about the Pumpkin, and the more she recalled, the more difficult the task in front of them appeared to be.

Molly stretched out her arm and fumbled about in the clothes that lay on a chair by the bedside; she presently drew forth the box of matches, Old Nancy's gift, and proceeded to examine this attentively, it being her first opportunity of doing so. Just an ordinary box of matches—at least, so it appeared—only there was no maker's name on the outside, simply a dark blue wrapper. There were a dozen matches inside—Molly counted. "I wonder if Jack has got the same number," she thought. Then hearing a distant clock strike seven, she put the match box back in her satchel and sprang out of bed.

While she was dressing she noticed that the bell which had been tolling solemnly when she fell asleep was now silent.

When Molly was ready to go downstairs she climbed on a chair and looked out of the window into the street below, which was already alive with people moving to and fro on their early morning

business. Everything looked so clean and fresh,
and the sun was shining, and a breeze greeted Molly,
so warm and sweetly scented that all the little
doubts and fears that had crowded in on her, trying
to cloud her naturally sunny outlook, were suddenly
swept clean away, and Molly felt that everything was
possible and good on such a perfect morning. She
jumped lightly to the ground and ran across the
room humming.

A patch of sunshine lay on the floor by the
door, and as Molly stopped for a second to do up
her shoelace she saw a curious shadow form on
the patch. And the shadow was shaped like a
pumpkin! Startled, she looked hastily over her
shoulder: but there was nothing there. And even
as she looked again at the sunlit patch, the shadow
passed away.

"Why, it must have been only a cloud, passing
before the sun," she told herself, relieved. "How
silly of me."

But, nevertheless, she felt suddenly depressed;
she did not hum any more and she walked slowly
downstairs, instead of running with her usual quick
step. In passing Jack's room, the door of which

Aunt Janet Puts on her Bonnet

stood wide open, she saw that the room was empty. So Jack had raced her, and was already downstairs.

"Yes, he's been up this last half-hour, and he's out in the back garden now," Aunt Janet informed her. "Did you sleep well, dearie? Run out and tell your brother breakfast'll be ready in three minutes, will you, dearie?"

And Aunt Janet bustled about between the pantry and the fireplace and the breakfast table, in the little back room. A very tempting breakfast table it looked, too; set for five, and everything so spick and span, from the crisp brown rolls to the long glass vase filled with yellow flowers standing in the centre of the white cloth.

So Molly went in search of Jack, through the open back door into the garden. The garden which was long and narrow, was full of bushes and flowers and little winding paths. At the farthest end stood six tall elm trees in a row, and it was here that Molly spied Jack and Glan's father, standing, talking earnestly together.

"Hullo, Molly," called Jack, when he saw her. "Come and look here."

Knock Three Times!

Molly made her way down the garden, and saw that Jack and the old man were both gazing down at something at the foot of one of the trees. It was a dark red plant-pot filled with dry soil.

"Mr—er—*he* was just telling me—what do you think, Molly?" said Jack excitedly. "The Black Leaf came up in this plant-pot one year!"

"Oh," Molly gasped, and gazed at the pot with awe. Such an ordinary plant-pot it looked, with nothing at all about it to suggest that it had ever been connected with any magic.

"Of course, missie," Glan's father explained mournfully, "it was no use me a-picking it that year, you see, because there was no Pumpkin to pick it for. Besides," he added bitterly, "it on'y came up for spite. That's all — pure spite, I call it—just to taunt me as it were. I couldn't bide the sight of it—especially as the Pumpkin was out of reach—in—in *your* World."

"What would have happened if you *had* picked it?" asked Jack.

"Nothing would have happened. At the end of the thirteen days it would have withered away, and the plant might not have come up again, per-haps—but I don't know about that. Still, if it hadn't, what should we have done this year when we do want it? Eh?"

"Yes," said Molly. "It is a good job you didn't pick it, because, supposing it didn't come up again—I suppose there would have been no hope of getting rid of the Pumpkin this time?"

"Unless Old Nancy had discovered another spell," suggested Jack.

The old man shook his head dismally, and ran his fingers through his beard.

"No," he said. "I had a feeling—in my bones—that we should need the Black Leaf some day. I always said the Pumpkin would return from—from *your* World. And then—and then those dreams I had——"

"Oh, why didn't the Leaf come up in your plant-pot this year!" sighed Molly.

"Things never happen like that," mumbled Glan's father.

"They do sometimes," said Molly.

But the old man only shook his head.

"There's Aunt Janet calling us to breakfast," said

89

Molly. "I was sent out to fetch you. Come along!"
And she led the way back indoors again, followed by
the other two.

"Now, what have you been doing in the garden?"
cried Aunt Janet, catching sight of the three serious
faces. "Looking at that old plant-pot again, I'll be
bound. You ought to be ashamed of yourself,"
she said, shaking her head at Glan's father. "Brooding over that miserable old pot—before breakfast, and
on such a lovely morning too. If I had my way I'd
smash the ugly old thing up and have done with it—
though really I believe you enjoy it"—she disregarded
the old man's reproachful glance, and clapped some
plates on the table a little impatiently. "What good
does it do, brooding over things that are past and
gone and can't be helped! It's the future we can
help, and it's the future we should give our thought
to, and make it better than the past. Glan! Glan!
Where's Glan! Call Glan, somebody. He's in the
shop!"

But Glan had heard, and appeared at that moment
through the glass-windowed door that led from the
parlour to the shop.

"Good-morning all, good-morning," he cried,
90

beaming and rubbing his hands together. "What a perfect morning, to be sure. And did the little lady and her brother rest well after the strenuous time they had yesterday?"

"Very well, thank you," said Molly.

"Slept like a top," said Jack.

"Ah, that's right," said Glan, taking his place at the table, round which the others were already seated. "And what is this our good Aunt has provided? Scrambled eggs! Excellent, excellent indeed. What a perfect morning. Who could feel sad at heart on a day like this!"

He seemed in great spirits, and started to hum as he helped himself to salt, while his father rolled his eyes up leaving only the whites visible, to signify his despair at the incurable cheerfulness of his son.

"Come, come now, and how is father this morning?" Glan continued, pushing his father's chair closer to the table and tucking a serviette under his father's chin, for all the world as if he were a baby in a high chair.

"He's been at that old plant-pot again," said Aunt Janet.

Knock Three Times!

"Bad wicked man," smiled Glan, wagging his spoon at his Father, who received all Glan's bantering remarks with the same stolid expression, and without the flicker of a smile. Jack marvelled at Glan's perseverance with his Father, when his attempts to cheer him up were always without success. He began to doubt whether the old man *could* smile, and tried to imagine him doing so—but failed.

"After breakfast," said Glan, "if he is very good and promises not to pick the currants out of the buns, Father shall mind the shop while the little lady and her brother, and Aunt Janet, and yours faithfully, put on their best bonnets with the bead trimmings, and their elastic-sided boots, and brown cotton gloves"—he gave an elaborate wink at Aunt Janet—"and sally forth to learn what plans are afoot, and to find out what portion of the country we are each to search."

"Will Jack and I be allowed to go together?" asked Molly, anxiously.

"Certainly, if you wish," said Glan.

"Of course we'd rather, wouldn't we, Moll?" said Jack.

92

Aunt Janet Puts on her Bonnet

And she assented quickly, hoping at the same time that now they would probably both win — or fail together.

When breakfast was finished, and while Aunt Janet went to put on her bead-trimmed bonnet, and elastic-sided boots, and brown cotton gloves, Glan showed the two children over the shop. It contained a most tempting array of sugared cakes and buns and pastries and bread—all of which Glan told them he made himself, in the bakehouse at the side of the shop. The shop was sweet and clean, like the rest of the house, and the sight of Glan, in his white cap and overall, standing behind the counter and beaming cheerfully around him was a sight to lighten the heart of anyone—except Glan's father.

"It's fortunate that your Father can look after the place while you are out," remarked Molly. "But I thought you said he was taken back and given a place at Court, didn't you? I thought that was why he wore a velvet robe and keys."

"Quite right," said Glan, "but it is only a very unimportant position. You see, he's getting old— he only has to turn up at Court every Tuesday and Friday. It keeps him amused. On his free days he does all sorts of things to fill up his time. . . . Ah, here he comes," he continued, as his Father shuffled into the shop. " Now, be very careful, Father, and look after everything nicely while we're away, won't you? And here—you'd better wear this or you'll spoil that lovely velvet robe."

And Glan whipped off his white apron and made his Father put it on. This, over his gorgeous velvet robe, gave him a comical appearance which was by no means lessened by the melancholy expression on his face. Glan gave a chuckle. With arms akimbo he surveyed his Father with his head on one side, then he chuckled again. Such an irresistible, infectious chuckle it was that Jack and Molly, despite their efforts not to, started to laugh. Glan went on chuckling and laughing, and once having started the three of them continued laughing and could not stop, until the tears came into their eyes, and Jack had a stitch in his side, and Aunt Janet appeared, all ready to start, to see what all the noise was about.

" Poor old Father . . . it's too bad to laugh . . . but really . . . really . . ." and Glan dried his eyes on the sleeve of his white overall, and started to laugh again.

But Glan's Father could see nothing to laugh at, and had continued dusting the scales slowly and methodically all the time.

"These jam puffs are two a penny, aren't they?" he asked, quite unconscious of the figure he presented.

"Does your Father ever laugh?" Jack asked, as soon as they were outside the shop.

"Never to my knowledge," said Aunt Janet, "and I've kept house for him these twenty years."

"I've seen him smile—twice—as far as I can remember," replied Glan. "But that was a long time ago. . . . Perhaps he'll *laugh* one of these days—when we find the Black Leaf?"

They made their way down the street and into the market square, which presented a very different appearance in the daylight from the sleepy, peaceful look it had worn last night in the moonlight. Now it was awake and all was bustle and hurry, with shops open, and people passing to and fro.

95

Knock Three Times!

"Where did you say we were going first?" asked Jack.

"I didn't say," said Glan, "but I should think you might guess by Aunt Janet's bonnet that it's somewhere very special."

"We're going to the Palace, dearies," Aunt Janet broke in.

"To the Palace!" exclaimed the children.

"And shall we see the King?" Molly added.

"Of course," said Glan.

At this moment their attention was attracted by the sound of people running and shouting, and they saw that a big crowd was rapidly gathering round the market cross. "What is it?" "What's the matter?" people near by were asking each other, and unable to get information they would rush off and join the jostling, excited mob in order to find out for themselves.

"Wait here a moment," said Glan, "and I'll go and see. Don't follow me or we shall lose each other in the crowd. I won't be long."

And leaving the children and Aunt Janet standing outside a quaint little tea-shop, he dashed forward and was quickly lost to sight in the surging mass of people that were rushing onward to the market cross. Everyone was simmering with excitement, and Jack and Molly had great difficulty in obeying Glan's instructions to wait outside for him there, especially whenever a shout or groan of sympathy or indignation rose above the murmuring of the crowd, and told them that something unusual was taking place.

But they waited, and in a few minutes they saw Glan making his way back through the outskirts of the crowd. He hurried toward them, his face unusually grave.

"Come along," he said, taking each of the children by an arm and hastening them away before they could ask any questions; and he signed to Aunt Janet, who followed behind them as quickly as possible. "Don't look back. It's no use. We can't do anything to help. It's one of the Pumpkin's victims, some poor fellow caught by him outside the City walls."

"What has he done to him?" Jack managed to gasp out.

"Made both his arms disappear, and covered his face with a horrible grey stain. The man looks

97

Knock Three Times!

awful. I'm glad you didn't see him — we can do nothing to help . . . except one thing," said Glan.

"The Black Leaf?" asked Molly.

"The only thing," said Glan.

CHAPTER IX

Planning the Search

THEY turned out of the square into a wide avenue, bordered on each side with beautiful trees. At the end of this avenue stood the Palace gates, and behind these, glimpses could be caught of the Palace itself, gleaming white through the trees and bushes which surrounded it and almost hid it from sight of the gates; the only parts which were entirely visible were its four white towers which rose high above the tree tops. Having ascended the flight of wide, marble steps before the gates, the four visitors passed the sentry—who seemed to know Glan quite well—and made their way through the grounds to the main entrance of the Palace.

Jack and Molly were lost in admiration of the beauty of the scene before them. The creeper-clad walls and white towers of the Palace stood in well-wooded grounds through which a little river wandered, sparkling in the sunlight. Along the central avenue that led to the Palace, and up the

99

great wide steps to the main door, there moved a constant stream of people, dressed in all sorts of lovely shades and colours; from a distance you might almost think they were the moving reflections of the flowers that clustered in profusion wherever your eyes turned. Had this been really so, Glan in his white suit might have passed for the reflection of a white stock, perhaps; Molly for a blue and white periwinkle; Jack for a dark blue hyacinth; and Aunt Janet, who was all in brown, for a large autumn leaf.

They joined the moving procession, and as they began to mount the steps Glan explained to the children that all these people were on the same errand as themselves; they had come to offer their help in the organized search that was about to take place. The main doors of the Palace were soon reached and they passed through, and were presently ushered into a spacious hall, panelled with dark oak. (For although the outsides of the buildings in the City were white, the children had already noted that the insides were coloured in many and varied styles.)

The hall was already crowded with people, and

on a raised daïs at the far end there sat the King's Councillors—a group of wise and learned men and women — round a long table. At first Jack and Molly could not see very well, but when a sudden hush fell on the assembly and the people all bowed, the children could see over the bowed heads that some one of importance was entering. They were made sure of this by the nudges of Aunt Janet. And looking up they saw it was the King.

His Majesty was middle-aged and rather tall and well built, and had a strong, clean-shaven face. The children liked his appearance. That he was 'every inch a king' could truly be said of him, though he wore no crown or velvet robes as the kings usually did in the children's story-books at home, but was dressed very simply in a suit that reminded Jack vaguely of an admiral's uniform.

"What a decent sort he looks," whispered Jack to Molly.

After a few words of welcome to the people the King called upon one of the Councillors—a shrewd little man with tufty white whiskers—to tell the true story of the Pumpkin's return to the Possible World, which the Councillor did, having obtained a full account from Old Nancy. The only question which still remained unsolved was: Who was the traitor who had drugged Old Nancy, and so aided the Pumpkin to return? This mystery, he said, they hoped to clear up when the Black Leaf was found.

When he had finished his story and had sat down, a buzz of murmuring voices filled the hall, and people turned to one another commenting on the story about Old Nancy which they had just been told, and comparing notes on the exaggerated versions of the tale that had reached them from various quarters.

Silence fell as the King rose again. After a few comments on the Pumpkin's return, he began to speak of the plans for searching, which he and the Councillors had discussed at an emergency meeting early this morning.

"To make sure that every likely inch of ground is searched," he said, "we have taken a map of the City and the outlying country, as far as the boundaries of this kingdom extend—and this is the only kingdom in which the Black Leaf can grow, remember—and we have divided this map into a number of small squares. Now what we want you each to do is to choose a square of the map, which you may take away with you—and search thoroughly every inch of the ground marked.

" In this way the Black Leaf must be found sooner or later—unless there is any careless searching or delay in searching. For, remember, we have only *eleven days left* before the Black Leaf disappears—and if it is not found before then the Pumpkin will remain with us for a year until the Leaf appears again and another search can be made.

"Those who volunteer outside the City are advised to search in couples, as the Pumpkin will be a constant source of danger to a person alone, whereas, if there are two of you, one can always keep watch while the other searches difficult places, or rests for a while."

And here the King said a special word of warning regarding decoys and traps set by the Pumpkin in order to hinder the searchers, and then went on to explain what should be done if the Black Leaf was found, repeating the words that Jack and Molly had already heard from Old Nancy.

"As soon as it is known that the Black Leaf is found," the King continued, "signals will be given throughout the country, so that all the searchers can cease, and make their way back to the City and the hill by Old Nancy's cottage, in order to witness the Pumpkin's punishment. These signals will be given by means of beacon fires which will be lit on the hill tops near and far. And when the glad news reaches the City all the bells will be set ringing."

"Your Majesty, would it be possible for one of the Pumpkin's friends to start the first beacon blazing, before the Leaf was found, in order to stop the searchers?" some one in the hall inquired.

"No," replied the King. "Because we are so arranging it that only the person who has actually plucked the Black Leaf, and has it in his or her hand, can set a light to the first beacon. Each beacon is being specially guarded . . . well, I will admit that we have called in the aid of Old Nancy to help us in the guarding of them. So you may rest assured that none of the Pumpkin's friends will be able to touch the beacons. . . . So, whoever finds the Black Leaf, remember to set the nearest beacon on fire before starting back to Old Nancy, that we may all know the good news at the earliest possible moment."

The King concluded by asking for volunteers to search outside the City and inside the City to come

Planning the Search

forward and sign their names in the book which had been placed on a table half-way along the hall.

"The Pumpkin has already, in the last few hours, caused much sorrow," he said sadly. "Let us make certain that this is the last time he shall ever bring disaster and misery to our country. Let us put our best efforts into this scheme for finding the Black Leaf, and so banish for all time the Grey Pumpkin."

He sat down amid a great cheer which came from the hearts of the people in the crowded hall. It was obvious that the King was very popular. The people pressed forward eagerly to sign their names, and Jack and Molly together with Glan and Aunt Janet were among the foremost to signify their willingness to help. Both the children caught the wave of enthusiasm which swept through the hall, and felt that here was a country and a King well worth working for. And their dislike of the Pumpkin who would spoil everything grew more intense.

"I'm afraid I can only volunteer to search inside the City," said Aunt Janet to the children as they turned away from the table. "I can't walk very far without getting a bit tired. And as for running—I couldn't—not if fifty Pumpkins were after me."

105

"I think it's jolly sporty of you to offer at all," said Jack.

"Oh, we all want to do what we can, dearie," she smiled.

The four of them moved on and joined a group of people who were examining one of the large maps of the City and surrounding country which were hanging round the room. They had begun to discuss what part of the country would be the best for them to search, when they heard, much to their surprise, someone call out the names of the two children in a loud voice. Turning quickly they saw that the King had the big book of names in front of him, and with his finger to a name on the page, was looking round the room. It was one of the Councillors near him who had called out their names, evidently at the King's request. Before the children could wonder what they ought to do, the King spoke:

"I see," he said, "that we have two friends from the Impossible World who have kindly offered to help us. I should like to thank them personally. Strangers are often lucky!"

Some one started a cheer which was quickly taken up by the entire hall full of people, and Jack and

Planning the Search

Molly, both blushing furiously at this unexpected attention, were pushed forward by Glan and Aunt Janet, to the foot of the raised daïs where the King greeted them, welcoming them to the country, and warmly shaking hands with them. They chatted together for a few minutes, the King asking many questions about the Impossible World.

"But, ah me!" the King said. "I am afraid this will be the Impossible World now that the Pumpkin's returned."

"We will soon make it Possible again, your Majesty," said Molly. "If it is in our power to do so."

"I'm sure we shall all do our best," said the King. "Now which part of the country would you prefer to search?"

The children said they did not mind, as all the country was strange and fresh to them, and asked his Majesty if he thought the Leaf was more likely to be outside the City than inside.

"Of course, one can never be sure, but I think it's much more likely to be outside the City than inside," the King replied. "But still it *may* be inside! We shall make a thorough search inside, naturally:

in every garden, and street, and plant-pot, and window-box—everywhere, in every place likely and unlikely."

When the children heard that the Leaf was more likely to be outside they at once made up their minds. Outside the City walls they would search, Jack and Molly together. And so it was arranged.

They chose a little square of the country that lay outside the East Gate of the City. It was entirely fresh country to them, and Molly liked the names given to that part of the country. Down the Three Green Lanes, over Goblin's Heath, through the Orange Wood, and the country along the banks of a broad river to Lake Desolate, and the Brown Hills. Although these names were all marked in one little square on the map it was really a good many miles—especially when every likely part must be carefully gone over and examined.

After Jack and Molly had received their small square of map, Glan stepped forward to pick his square. He shook hands and chatted with the King for a second, and then stood before the map trying to make up his mind. While he was deciding, tracing along the map with his plump white fore-

Planning the Search

finger, the children stood aside watching the stream of people passing to and fro, choosing their square of map, shaking hands with the King, and passing on and out of the great door at the end of the hall. Most of them had a friendly smile and nod for Jack and Molly as they went by, and several came up to the children, and shook hands with them, thanking them for offering to help their country in this trouble.

At length, after Glan had chosen, and helped Aunt Janet to choose her bit, and shaken hands excitedly with everybody round about (including Aunt Janet, by mistake), he, Aunt Janet, Jack, and Molly bade farewell to the King and made their way out of the Palace. They retraced their steps through the Palace grounds, passing the sentry at the gate, and went toward the Market Square again. Glan and Aunt Janet insisted on showing the children the way to the East Gate, and so the four went along talking eagerly, the children full of enthusiasm for the coming search, for the King, and for the Possible World.

"I've got a big forest to search in my bit," said Glan. "I like forests. And I'm arranging for father

to help me if he feels inclined—on the days when he's
not at Court. I wish I could have got a bit to search
outside the East Gate—so as to be near you both—
but all the bits I wanted were already taken by other
people. Fortunately, though, I've managed to get a
square that backs on to a piece of the ground you'll
be searching—though I start from the West Gate.
You see the wood bends round at this point——"
and he compared his square of map with Jack
and Molly's square, and showed them where his
ground touched theirs. "So I shan't be so very
far away," he laughed. "You can't get rid of me,
altogether."

"I'm sure we don't want to," said Molly.

"Rather not," said Jack.

"Oh, Glan, you will be careful, won't you?—and
not get caught by the Pumpkin?" added Molly
anxiously.

"Of course, little lady," Glan replied. "You
should see me *run* if I want to. I'll not get caught."
He was still studying and comparing the maps.
"Why, look here!" he exclaimed, "you've got the
Orange Wood in your bit. Well, I never! D'you
hear that, Aunt Janet? The Orange Wood. . . .

Planning the Search

We've got a relative who lives in that wood. I must give you his name." Glan scribbled something on a piece of paper and handed it to the children. "Any of the people in the village near by will direct you to his house—they all know him. Papingay's his name—I've written it down, you see. He'll be delighted to see you—tell him you know us, Aunt Janet and Father and me. But don't be surprised at his funny little ways—he's a queer old soul—a very queer old soul." Glan chuckled to himself at some recollection.

"He's a kind of cousin of Glan's father, dearies," observed Aunt Janet.

The children were glad to hear of this one person, at any rate, whom they might trust in the strange, unknown country before them.

"Be sure to humour him, though," added Glan. "He's worth it. Don't forget."

While they had been talking they had been passing through many quaint streets on their way to the East Gate: streets that on an ordinary occasion would have made Jack and Molly long to stop and explore them slowly, there were so many tempting and curious things to be seen. But there was no time for loitering now. There was serious work to be done. So they hastened along until at length the East Gate was reached.

Here Glan produced two neat little boxes of sandwiches and cakes, giving one of them to Jack and one to Molly. "A snack for lunch," he said.

"You're sure to find plenty of friends as you go along," said Aunt Janet. "But do take care of yourselves, dearies. Good luck be with you." And she fumbled for her pocket-handkerchief and dabbed her eyes rapidly, while Glan patted her on the shoulder.

"Here's to our next meeting," he cried cheerily, "and may it be soon. Who's going to light the first beacon, little lady, you or I?"

"Neither," said Jack, laughing. "I am."

"That's the sort," cried Glan, patting Aunt Janet vigorously, as he beamed at Jack.

The keeper of the East Gate had by this time appeared and was cautiously opening the gate. Finding the way clear he opened it wide.

"Laugh at misfortune," Glan shouted gaily, as Jack and Molly passed out on to the High Road.

Planning the Search

"Keep up a good heart, and — tss — remember — we shall win. Good luck! Good luck!" They saw him wave his white cap in the air; there was a flutter of brown-gloved hands, then the gate closed.

CHAPTER X

Some One Meets Jack and Molly in the Third Green Lane

THEY had gone but a short distance along the broad white road which led to the Three Green Lanes (according to the map), when they heard the East Gate of the City open and shut again with a clang, and looking back Jack and Molly saw that two people had come out and had started off in the opposite direction to that in which they were going.

"Two more searchers," said Jack. "I remember that little man with the green coat, don't you, Molly? He was at the Palace—had very twinkling eyes."

"Oh, yes, I saw him," said Molly. "And that boy with him in that curious red-brown suit. I wonder which part they are searching. Supposing *they* are the lucky people who are going to find the Black Leaf . . . if we only knew," sighed the little girl, standing in the middle of the white road and gazing pensively at the two figures in the distance.

"I know one thing," said Jack. "We shan't be the lucky people if we don't move along. Come on, Molly."

Two minutes' brisk walking brought them to the entrance to the First Green Lane. And here their search began. The lane was a very twisty one, and was closed in on either side with high thick hedges; fresh and green the hedges were, and starred with tiny white flowers that smelled very sweet.

"How strange that it isn't autumn here, like it was at home," said Jack. "It's more like summer here, isn't it, Molly?"

"It isn't really strange," said Molly. "Everything is so different here, isn't it? I don't see why the seasons in the Possible World should be like ours any more than anything else is like ours."

"No. P'r'aps you're right," agreed Jack.

They went carefully along, searching thoroughly as they went, Molly taking the left-hand side of the lane and Jack the right. For the most part it was fairly easy work; there were not many places in the First Green Lane where the Black Leaf could grow

115

undetected, though from time to time an extra thick and low-spreading bush would necessitate a halt for a thoroughly satisfactory examination.

"There is one thing that seems strange to me," Molly went on presently. "And that is the way the ordinary and the magic things seem to all get mixed up together. I'm sure I shall be forgetting, when we get home again, and keep expecting spells and magic things to happen."

"So shall I," said Jack; and then, as Molly began to laugh—"What's the matter?" he asked.

"Oh, Jack," she laughed. "What would Aunt Phoebe say if she could see us now!"

"'I'm sure I don't know what the world's coming to,'" mimicked Jack, in an Aunt Phoebe voice, and then joined in Molly's laughter. "And the best of it is," he chuckled, "it's all through her giving you that birthday present. She *would* be wild."

"I suppose we really ought not to laugh at her," laughed Molly. "It's hardly respectful—but, somehow, I can't just help it."

They continued to search, chatting and laughing, in a light-hearted, excited mood, and soon they had covered the best part of the First Green Lane. As

116

they neared the end—a break in the hedge (on Jack's side) blocked by a white gate revealed a big field which lay behind the hedge.

"Hullo," said Jack. "Have we got to search this field, too, I wonder. Where's the map?"

Molly had it in her pocket, and produced it at once. Leaning against the gate the two children studied it carefully.

"Yes. See. Here it is . . . marked here," said Molly. "The hedge on the left-hand side—the side I was searching—is the boundary; but the field this side is marked in our square."

"I tell you what then," suggested Jack. "I'll start on the field while you finish to the end of the lane—it's only a few yards more. Then you come back and start the other end of the field."

Molly agreed, so they separated for a few minutes and continued the search. But there was no sign of the Black Leaf anywhere in the big field or in the First Green Lane, and at length they started on the Second Green Lane.

The Second Green Lane had low hedges and many ferns and wild flowers growing by the way, and a ditch running along one side of it, which made

117

the searching a little more difficult. There were also several gates leading from this lane into fields which had to be searched too. Some of the fields where the grass was long took a good time to do properly. But the two children stuck to it perseveringly, urged on by the hope that perhaps just round the corner, or behind the next tree, or even, perhaps, a few feet ahead of them among the long grass, grew that which they sought—the Black Leaf. But so far they had searched in vain.

In the early afternoon they found themselves at the beginning of the Third Green Lane; and here they decided to stop and have a short rest and some lunch. When they sat down on the soft grass by the side of the lane they suddenly discovered that they were really tired; and when they saw the tempting little sandwiches and cakes in the "snack for lunch" packets Glan had given them they realized that they were really hungry. They had been too busy and excited to realize these things before. Over lunch they got out the map again and studied it.

"What a lonely piece of country this seems," Jack remarked. "Do you know, we haven't seen a single person since we started searching!"

118

Some One Meets Jack & Molly

"Nor a single house," said Molly. "It's a good thing we have this map with us. How useful it is. . . . Let me look, Jack. Are there any houses or villages marked near here, because we shall have to find some place to stay to-night if possible."

"There seems to be some sort of village marked there . . . um . . . it's not very near, though," said Jack. "It's the other side of the Goblin's Heath. . . . There doesn't seem to be a house of any sort marked between here and that village, does there? Still, I daresay we could reach the village before dusk, if we are not delayed at all——"

"And if the Heath isn't too big——"

"If it is and we can't find a cottage before the end of the Heath, we'll climb up a tree, Moll. It'll be great sport. And we shall be quite safe there till daylight."

They packed up the remains of the lunch, for it was a very generous "snack" that Glan had put in for each of them, and after resting a few minutes longer they rose to their feet and prepared to start on again.

"My word, I am thirsty," said Jack. At Molly's advice he tried one of the little sweet things in Old

Nancy's packet, and though it was certainly refreshing Jack still craved for a drink of water. " Is there a stream of water marked anywhere near here. Give me the map again, Molly."

They were standing at the beginning of the Third Green Lane with the map in their hands, when the sound of some one singing came to them from a distance.

Jack and Molly looked at each other. This was the first human sound they had heard since they left the High Road. Perhaps this person, whoever it was, could tell them where they could get some water. The singer was evidently approaching, as the song grew louder and clearer, from the direction of the lane which they were just about to search. Then, just as they expected the singer to come round the corner of the lane—the singing ceased abruptly— and no one appeared.

Jack and Molly waited a while, then started off down the lane in the direction whence the singing had come, thinking perhaps that the singer had stopped to rest round the corner of the lane. They were right. As they turned the corner they saw someone sitting under a tree at the side of the lane.

Some One Meets Jack & Molly

It was a young girl, a little older than Jack and Molly—such a pretty girl, with grey-green eyes and a straight, white nose, and deep golden hair that curled about her shoulders. Her soft green frock matched the colour of her eyes.

She did not notice Jack and Molly at first, as her attention was taken up by the contents of a small wicker basket in her lap: she was peering inside it anxiously, and counting aloud.

"Eight, nine, ten," they heard her say. "Eleven. . . . Oh, dear, I've lost . . . no, here it is . . . twelve. Oh, that's right!"

She looked up, and saw the children. She gazed up at them, then smiled (such a friendly, sweet smile, Molly thought).

"Oh, I . . . I didn't hear you come along," she said.

"We heard you singing," said Molly.

The girl blushed. "I didn't know anyone was near," she said. "I often sing when I'm by myself —it's so lonely, as a rule." She fastened the lid of her basket down.

"We were awfully glad to hear you," said Jack. "Because, do you know, we haven't met a soul since we left the East Gate."

Knock Three Times!

"Have you come from the City, then?" asked the girl with much interest, rising to her feet. "Oh, you can't imagine how lonely it is to live out here. What news is there? What does the City look like now? Oh, I'd give anything to live in the City with crowds of people and lights and shops and—and real pavement."

"Haven't you got any pavement then in the village where you live?" asked Jack.

"I don't live in a village," answered the girl. "It's right out here in all this lonely part that mother and I live."

"Near here?" asked Molly.

"Yes. Just at the end of the Third Green Lane," said the girl.

"In a house?" inquired Jack.

"Yes. Why not?" the girl smiled. "What did you think we'd live in?"

"I meant," said Jack, "it's not marked on our map; there's no house marked until you get to the other side of the Goblin's Heath, and I didn't think there was one so close."

The girl began to laugh. "Well, there is one, even if it isn't marked on your map. They don't mark all the houses, you know. If your way takes you along down this lane you'll pass the house, and mother would be awfully pleased to see you if you could spare a little while. She rarely gets news of the City or sees anybody."

"We *were* going along this way," said Jack. "And we were just wondering if there was anywhere we could get a drink of water, because we're both so thirsty. . . ."

"Thirsty?" said the girl. "Why, here is the very thing!" And she opened her basket and took out a beautiful bunch of grapes. "I had been sent out to gather these from our vine—twelve bunches I've gathered. Do have one." She placed a delicious-looking bunch in Jack's hands.

"Oh, no—really. I say, can you spare them, though?" protested Jack. "And wouldn't your mother mind?"

"She'd mind if I didn't give you a bunch when you were so thirsty," said the girl, and insisted on Molly having a bunch too.

"Well, it really is awfully kind of you," said Jack, and Molly thanked her also.

Molly hesitated just a second before eating her grapes, wondering if they were doing right in accepting them from the little girl whose name even they didn't know. But a glance at the little girl's sweet, frank face reassured any doubts Molly may have had. Jack had already started his bunch. So Molly ate her grapes too.

"You know," said Jack, "I don't think I've ever tasted such jolly fine grapes. I was terribly thirsty after searching all the morning."

"Searching?" asked the girl, puzzled. "Did you say searching? What have you lost?"

"It isn't what we've lost—it's what we can't find," said Jack. "You know—it's what they're all looking for."

The girl shook her head. "I don't know what you mean," she said.

"Don't you know about the search for the Black Leaf?" asked Jack in surprise. "Oh, I say. And about the Pumpkin being back again—of course, you know that?"

"What!" screamed the girl. "The Pumpkin back? No! No! I didn't know that. We hear nothing—living out here alone. . . . But, oh dear, oh dear! Whatever are we going to do?" She was trembling and seemed very upset. "I must get home at once and tell mother—poor mother," she added. She fastened the lid of her basket with shaking fingers. "Are you coming along this way now?"

The children explained to her that although they were coming that way they would have to search as they came, and advised her to go on in front of them to tell her mother if she felt this was the wisest thing to do. But she seemed afraid to leave them.

"I'd rather stay with you, if you don't mind," she said. "I—I expect you'll think I'm an awful coward—but I simply daren't go on alone. I'll help you search as we go along; and do tell me how it all happened—how the Pumpkin came back."

So, as the three of them moved off down the lane, Jack and Molly recounted something of what had happened. They did not talk much about themselves, but related the main incidents of the Pumpkin's return. Their companion listened eagerly, putting in a hurried question every now and then. When they had finished she said:

"Well, I do think it's plucky of you. To search like this—in a strange land. I—I feel quite ashamed of myself for being so scared just now. We all have to take our chance. Do let me help you search this

125

bit of lane. And afterward, I'll go to the City and ask to be given a part to search too. How far do you intend to search to-day?"

"We thought of trying to get as far as the other side of the Goblin's Heath," said Jack.

"Oh, you'll never be able to do that before night-fall!" the girl exclaimed. "It's a very big Heath. I wonder—would you care to stay at our house to-night? Mother and I would be only too proud to have you, if you'd care. . . ."

"It's very good of you," said Molly. "Per-haps——"

"Well, wait until you see mother, if you'd prefer that," said the girl. "Wait until you see our house. I know I shouldn't care to promise to stay with anyone until I'd seen where they lived. In a strange country too."

She had added this, seeing that Jack and Molly hesitated. But they were more than half-persuaded, because she spoke so reasonably and frankly.

They continued to search the Third Green Lane thoroughly; the afternoon wore on, and the shadows of eventide began to fall.

Presently the girl said, "We are near the end of

the lane now. Round the next turning you will see my house."

So far the search had been in vain, and Jack and Molly were beginning to feel very tired, as the lane had been long and difficult.

"We must have been two hours searching this lane," said Molly. "Will your mother be getting anxious about you?"

The girl shook her head. "And she won't even be cross when she sees that I've brought visitors home with me. You will come in, won't you?" she asked, "and we can all have tea together."

It sounded so tempting that the children accepted gladly, especially as the house hove in sight at that moment. Turning the corner they came suddenly upon it. Such a quaint, cosy little house, which lay snuggled away behind a cluster of thick bushes and trees. The lane continued for only a short distance beyond the house, then it opened out into a great wide heath—the Goblin's Heath. The children hadn't time to take in much of the scenery, as their companion ushered them into the garden of her house quickly. It was darker in the garden under the trees than out in the roadway, and they saw that a little light was

127

glimmering from one of the windows of the house, which made it look very homely and comfortable. Jack and Molly followed their companion up the path to the front door.

The girl tapped twice on the front door, then, rattling the handle and calling out, "Here we are, mother!" she threw open the door and the three of them passed in.

They found themselves in a dark, narrow passage, at the end of which they could see a glow as from firelight. Their companion closed the front door and led the way along the passage.

"Here we are, mother!" she called again, and a figure appeared in the firelit opening at the end of the passage, and stood there chuckling softly.

Suddenly, Jack and Molly were afraid.

"Jack, I'm going back!" gasped Molly, and turning, both the children made for the door. But it was shut fast, and there were no handles or bolts to be found.

The girl and the figure in the firelight burst into loud laughter.

"You little sillies!" a voice cried, accompanied by another burst of laughter.

Some One Meets Jack & Molly

They could see the girl in green quite plainly now. She had reached the end of the passage and stood whispering to the other person. The firelight shone on both of them. The girl in green was strangely altered. No longer fresh and young and pretty—her face looked old and hard and scornful. Jack and Molly caught a few of the words she was whispering.

"Oh, Jack," Molly sobbed. "They're the Pumpkin's friends. We're trapped!"

CHAPTER XI

Trapped

JACK and Molly clutched hold of each other tightly, while a feeling of despair rushed over them. How foolish, how very foolish, they had been to trust the girl! What awful thing could be going to happen to them now? they wondered. The whispered conversation between the two at the end of the passage ended in a loud burst of laughter and giggling; then the girl turned toward them and beckoned.

"Come on," she said, "and the quicker the better it will be for you. . . . No nonsense now," as the children did not move.

"How dare you!" Jack managed to say. "Open this door and let us out at once. You—you mean sneak!" His voice was shaky, but very determined.

"Oh, don't be silly," said the girl. "You've *got* to obey now—so you might just as well come— unless you'd like me to fetch you both?"

Trapped

"Heh! Heh!" laughed the figure behind her. "I'd like to see you fetch them—that I would!"

The laughter and the nameless threat underlying the words gave the children a creepy sensation all up and down their spines.

"Oh, let's go before she *fetches* us," cried Molly, and went forward, dragging Jack by the hand.

"That's sense," said the girl, and made room for them to pass out of the passage into the firelight.

They found themselves in a round, cave-like room, which was lit up by the dancing flames of a log fire. Afterward Jack and Molly could not remember seeing any furniture in the room—nothing but the fire and a stone-arched fireplace. They could not recall seeing any windows, but they remembered the floor, which was made of cobbles, because it was hard to walk on. The room appeared to have no ceiling, or else a very high one, at any rate no ceiling was visible; overhead all was drifting smoke and black gloom, like the entrance to a railway tunnel.

"Let's have a look at the pretty dears," said the figure beside the girl, moving forward, and Jack and Molly stood face to face with the ugliest old woman they had ever seen, in fact, had ever even imagined.

Knock Three Times!

Her clay-coloured face was a mass of deep wrinkles; her narrow, sunken eyes looked like two restless black beads, darting from side to side, as if to escape from the two slits of eyelids which imprisoned them. Her nose and chin curved towards each other, after the fashion of nut-crackers, and her otherwise toothless mouth had one long yellow fang always visible. A bright crimson scarf was wound round her head, like a turban, from which long wisps of jet black hair escaped and hung about her face.

As the children looked at her, she did a terrifying thing (which they quickly discovered was a constant habit of hers). The old woman's restless beady eyes became suddenly still, and she fixed upon the children in turn a piercing stare, gradually opening her eyes wider and wider and wider until they became two big round black balls encircled by saucers of white— great, staring, still eyes . . . then suddenly the lids snapped over them, and they were once more little darting black beads.

"Heh! Heh! Heh!" laughed the old woman. "What a surprise for yer, duckies, wasn't it, now?" And she thrust her face close to the children and leered unpleasantly. "Stoopid little baggages!" she

Trapped

added. "Far for better you'd stopped at home—meddlin' in what don't concern you. But we'll soon learn you to come a-meddlin'." She turned to the girl behind her. "All right," she said in an undertone. "I'd know 'em again. I've had a good look. When's *he* coming?"

"In about an hour, I expect," answered the girl. Then she dropped her voice and started whispering again.

The two children gazed into each other's frightened white faces, and a little sob escaped from Molly.

"Eh?" said the old woman. "What you say, ducky? . . . Nothing? . . . All right. Come along then, my pretties, come along and wait in the drorin'-room. His Excellency the Grey Pumpkin is not at home just at present, but he won't be long; oh, dear no, he won't be long. Step this way in the drorin'-room. He'll be *pleased* to see yer. Heh! Heh!"

Molly glanced despairingly at the girl in green, the girl who had been so friendly a short time before when they were outside in the lane. Molly held out her hands appealingly—but the girl only laughed.

Knock Three Times!

"Oh have you no pity?" cried Molly. "Do, *do* let us go. He'll never know—the Pumpkin need never know. And—and if there is anything we can do for you, I'm sure my brother and I will be only too pleased . . ."

"Would you even give up the search—and go straight back home?" asked the girl sharply.

Here, then, was their chance of escape. If they would promise—Molly looked at Jack. What would the Pumpkin do to Jack—to her—when he came? She shuddered. Then she thought of Old Nancy, and the King, and Glan, and she knew that what the girl asked of them was impossible. She and Jack exchanged glances again. They had decided. They would take their chance.

"Would you promise?" asked the girl.

"No," answered Jack and Molly together.

"Hurry up and push them in, then, mother." The girl turned away, dismissing the subject immediately.

The old woman, chuckling to herself, opened a door in the wall (which the children had not noticed before) and told them to follow her to the "drorin'-room" unless they wanted to be "fetched" there. So they followed her.

Trapped

It was pitch dark on the other side of the door, and the old woman called out to the girl in green to hold a light for them, which she did, standing in the doorway holding a flickering taper above her head. Jack and Molly followed the old woman along a short passage, down a flight of stone steps to a door at the bottom. She took a key from her pocket, and calling to the girl in green again, telling her to hold the light at the top of the steps, she fumbled at the lock, opened the door, and then, without more ado, she pushed Jack and Molly inside, and slammed the door on them. They heard her lock the door, then go shuffling up the steps, grumbling to herself. Then another door banged—and all was silent.

Jack and Molly were in absolute darkness, and could not see an inch in front of them. They dared not move, but stood still clinging hold of each other.

"Oh, Jack, why *did* we trust her?" sobbed Molly.

"How were we to know . . . she seemed so decent . . . the sneak!" said Jack. "Oh, can't we *do* anything, Molly?"

It was dreadful, just standing in the dark—waiting.

Knock Three Times!

They talked in low tones to each other for a while, wondering how long it would be before the Pumpkin arrived. Neither of them dared to speak of what he might do when he came. If—if anything happened to them, would any one miss them, and come in search of them——

And then Molly remembered.

"Jack!" she cried. "The matches! Old Nancy's matches!"

"Why ever didn't we think of them before?" exclaimed Jack.

Now was the time to use them, undoubtedly; for if ever there was a dark place where some light was needed. . . . Jack and Molly were fumbling eagerly in their satchels.

"Be careful, Jack," said Molly. "Don't drop any. Have you got yours yet? I have. Now I'll strike one—and see what happens."

Jack was still searching his satchel for his box of matches. Meanwhile Molly took a match out of her box and struck it.

The children were not quite sure what they had expected to happen, but they felt vaguely disappointed to see just an ordinary little flare of light spring out of the

Trapped

darkness. Just an ordinary little flickering match. Anyway, they could now see what sort of a place they were shut up in. It was a kind of underground cellar, small and square and high roofed, and except for a few old boxes in one corner, empty. The walls were damp and mouldy, the floor broken and uneven, and the place seemed full of cobwebs.

And then they realized that it was not quite an ordinary match. It burnt longer, and, strange to say, the rays from it were concentrating all in one direction—like a long thin streak of light—pointing. Jack and Molly quickly sensed this. But what was the light pointing at? The flame was directed straight toward the boxes in the corner.

The children crossed the cellar and examined the boxes. They looked like wooden sugar boxes; there were three of them; and they were all empty. Jack pulled them away from the wall, but there was nothing behind them.

Then Molly's match flickered—and went out.

"Here, I'll light one," said Jack. "I've got mine now."

So Jack lit one. Just the usual match flare at

first, but as soon as it burned up the light gathered together all on one side of the match as it were, a long streak pointing in the exactly opposite direction to where the boxes were, right over on the other side of the cellar. For a moment Jack doubted, wondering whether it was a sort of joke on him. But he and Molly followed the light quickly, and saw that it was concentrated on a spot, high up on the wall, near the roof.

"Look! quick!" said Molly. "There's an iron ring or handle or something up there."

"But how can we reach it?" began Jack.

And then they remembered what the first match had shown them, and hastily dragging the boxes across the floor, piled them one on top of the other underneath the ring in the wall. Then Jack's match went out.

Both children were now tremendously excited; and fearful lest the Pumpkin should come before they had finished their investigations, they moved as rapidly as possible. Molly lit the next match, while Jack clambered up to the top of the boxes. Her light pointed straight at the iron ring.

"It's a ring all right!" cried Jack. "But, oh,

138

Trapped

Moll, I can't quite reach it! Whatever shall we do?"

As the match pointed steadily at the ring, and offered no further suggestions, Molly climbed up to the top of the boxes too. Jack's remark was only too true; the ring was just out of reach, try as they would to touch it.

"I believe I could reach it if you could lift me up, Jack," said Molly.

"Right-o!" said Jack. And then Molly's match went out.

As it would be too difficult to hold a match while trying to reach the ring, and as Molly said she remembered just where the ring was on the wall, it was decided to pull the ring if possible, and then light a match, and see what had happened.

So Jack lifted Molly up, and after groping about on the wall with her hands for a few seconds, she caught hold of the ring.

"I've got it! Keep steady, Jack!" she cried, joyfully, and gave a vigorous tug at the iron ring. "Something's given way—it feels as if a sort of door's opened. All right, put me down now, Jack, and strike a match."

Knock Three Times!

Jack followed her directions, and by the light of the match they saw that a small square door had opened in the wall above their heads. The light from the match pointed straight through the opening. It looked like a narrow, dark tunnel beyond. Jack put his match down on the top of the boxes to see if it would give them sufficient light from there, but directly it left his hand it went out, so they decided to try to get into the tunnel before they lit up again, as it was too difficult to hold matches while scrambling through the little black opening. Jack hoisted Molly up first, and she managed to get through the door, and then she turned and reached down her hand to pull Jack up. It was rather an ordeal, doing all this in the dark, but at length it was safely accomplished and they were both inside the tunnel. Once through the door, although rather cramped, they found there was sufficient room to stand up, if they bent their heads.

They did not stop to close the door behind them, but, lighting another match, they scurried along the tunnel as fast as ever they could. The tunnel twisted and turned a good deal, and then began to slope gradually upward. Two more matches they were

Trapped

obliged to light before they came at length to a
standstill where the tunnel branched out in two
directions. The light pointed steadily to the left, so
they followed it. Another minute's rapid walking,
and they felt a rush of cool air, and when their match
spluttered and went out, they could see that the inky
darkness was thinning a little way ahead, and so they
did not light another match, but hastened onward
toward a glimmer of light in the distance. As they
drew nearer they saw that it was the end of the tunnel
and led out into the open air.

Jack and Molly moved cautiously when they came
to the end. They crept out, and found themselves in
the middle of a thick tangle of bushes. Through the
bushes they struggled and forced a way until they
at length came out on to a narrow footpath which
threaded its way in and out of a host of bushes and
trees. They began to run as soon as they were on
the footpath, though they did not know where they
were or where it would lead them : but they ran, and
continued to run, until they reached a wider path, and
saw that they were on a big open heath. They
paused to regain their breath and take their bearings.

It was night-time, but the moon which sailed overhead in a clear sky made everything almost as light as day. They were certainly on a heath of some sort.

"Why, of course," Jack gasped, very much out of breath, "this must be the Goblin's Heath!"

CHAPTER XII

The Goblin's Heath

THE Goblin's Heath, with its little crouching bushes and heather-clad hillocks, looked very beautiful in the moonlight. Here and there a tree rising up from the low bushes around it stood out clearly against the night sky. Toward the nearest big tree Jack and Molly made their way. It was a giant of a tree, with great gnarled trunk, and plenty of room among its lower branches for a little girl and boy to curl up and rest comfortably and safely, screened by its thick curtain of leaves.

Once they were safely hidden in the tree, Jack and Molly had time to talk matters over. They decided to stay where they were until daylight, when they could continue their search. They talked and planned for some time, and then, as their excitement wore off a little, they began to get very sleepy. Everything seemed quiet and still around them, but they would take no more risks that night, so decided to sleep in turns—one keeping watch, and

143

waking the other up at certain intervals, or if anything happened in the meantime. They had no idea what the time was, so they arranged their intervals by the moon. When the moon reached a certain place, Jack, who undertook the first watch (protesting that he wasn't tired), was to wake Molly up. So Molly went to sleep, after making Jack promise that he would wake her up if she showed any signs of falling out of the tree. Jack had a hard struggle to keep awake at first, but he managed it somehow, and after Molly had woken up and taken a turn at watching, and he had had a short, sound sleep, he felt much refreshed.

The time wore on and Jack was just starting his second watch, and Molly had fallen asleep again, when he heard a long rustle in one of the bushes down below. He leant forward, peering down through the branches; there was evidently something stirring inside the bush; the leaves rustled and shook, and then were thrust aside, and a queer little figure stepped out and stood on the broad footpath in the moonlight. It was a very small, quaint man, dressed in brown, with a pointed cap on his head; he gazed along the pathway for a

144

moment, then turned and scanned the Heath in the opposite direction.

Jack gave a start as something moved in the tree beside him. But it was only Molly, awake, and wide-eyed, staring down at the little brown man with absorbed attention.

A squeal of laughter came from among the bushes a short distance away, and the next second another little man came running over the grass to the waiting figure and started talking rapidly. Their voices were very tiny, and although the sounds floated clearly up to the listeners in the tree, the words were undistinguishable. While they watched a third little man appeared, accompanied by two quaint little women, dressed in brown skirts and shawls and brown bonnets. All at once it dawned on Jack and Molly who these little people were, with the tiny, thin, dancing legs, and the elfish faces. They were goblins. And, of course, the Heath was named after them. The children had not expected to see any goblins on the heath; they had certainly thought it a picturesque name to call this part of the country, but they had not expected any reason for the name. But behold! here before their eyes were real live goblins, the first goblins they had ever seen, and they watched them, surprised and curious. More goblins now began to appear on the scene; one after another they came, darting from behind bushes, sliding down the trunks of trees or dropping from the branches, racing along the footpath, skipping over the grass, until by and by it seemed as if there were tiny brown figures scurrying to and fro on every side, appearing and disappearing, here, there, in and out; the whole Heath seemed to be alive with goblins. Such a squeaking of tiny voices, a chinking of goblin laughter, and a pattering of feet; and the goblins seemed to be all so busy and important and in a feverish haste about nothing at all.

Presently the children noticed that one of the goblins had made his way to the foot of their tree and was very busy dragging and pushing aside a big stone. He moved it away at length and disclosed a small hole in the tree trunk, close to the ground. He bent down and crawled into the hole. A scrambling and scratching began inside the tree, that sounded, as the scrambling noise became louder and nearer, as if the goblin were climbing up to the top of the trunk.

"Oh, Jack, I believe he lives in this tree,"

The Goblin's Heath

whispered Molly. "What shall we do if he finds us up here?" You see, they were not quite sure whether the goblins were friends or enemies, or how they would be disposed to regard them.

However, they were soon to know, for a few seconds later, the scratching and scrambling having continued until it sounded close underneath where the children were crouching, the goblin popped its head up through a hole just beside Jack's right foot. The Goblin studied the sole of Jack's shoe attentively for a moment, then his gaze travelled to Jack, whom he eyed with mild astonishment. Then he caught sight of Molly, and transferred his attention to her. The children remained silent, not knowing what to say. They could tell nothing of the Goblin's attitude toward them from his surprised face. Then he spoke. His voice sounded very small and far away, but the children were glad to find that they could understand what he said.

"Are you real?" asked the Goblin.

"Of course we are," said Jack.

"What are you?" was the next question.

Molly started to explain, but she soon noticed that the Goblin was shaking his head, so she stopped.

Knock Three Times!

"No . . . there isn't really a place called the Impossible World, which you can reach through a tree in a forest," he said, as if confiding to them a sad truth. "It's only a story—a make-believe place—like Dreamland."

Molly was taken aback.

"Oh, but there *is* such a place," she affirmed. "We know there is—because we have come from there."

"I like to hear you say that—but I don't believe you," said the Goblin, candidly. "I wish I could. And I wish you *were* real, indeed I do."

"We *are* real," said Jack, warmly. "We're as real as anything. Why, it's you that is only—that people say are not—I mean——"

"What do you think we are, then, if you don't believe we are real people?" asked Molly, quickly, giving Jack a warning glance.

"Well, you may be only an optical illusion—I may think I see you, but you may not really be there," suggested the Goblin blandly, wagging his quaint little head from side to side. His head and two little hands clutching the edge of the hole were still the only parts visible of him.

148

The Goblin's Heath

The children gazed down at him. An optical illusion! This was indeed a horrible thought, and made Molly pinch herself to make sure she was really there. Then she laughed.

"We are as real as you are," she said. Then she had an inspiration. "As real as Old Nancy," she added, watching the Goblin closely.

His expression changed immediately, and a look of glad surprise crossed his face. "Why, do you know her?" he asked quickly.

"Rather," said Jack. "She's a friend of ours."

"Then I am a friend of yours," said the Goblin, climbing out of the hole and standing beside the children. "Whether you are real—or—or—whatever you are."

Their recent lesson in trusting people had made the children more cautious, and although they could see that they had no choice in their behaviour toward this little Goblin, as they were powerless to escape from the Heath with its swarms of goblins, yet they felt friendly disposed toward him for his own sake. He seemed quite genuine in his regard for Old Nancy, and very soon he was sitting in the tree beside them, chatting away and asking them all about themselves, and answering questions by the score.

They found that he knew that the Pumpkin had returned, one of his brother-goblins had brought the news. And they discovered also that the goblins were the Pumpkin's bitter enemies. Then they told him all about their search for the Black Leaf, and how they were to search the Heath when daylight came.

"You won't see any of us in the daytime," said the Goblin. "We'll be all asleep down our little holes . . . but I don't think the Black Leaf is anywhere on the Heath, or one of us would have seen it, and the news would have soon spread amongst us."

"Still, I suppose we shall have to search it all the same . . . as we promised," said Molly.

"Yes, you're quite right," agreed the Goblin, "Besides, we *might* not have seen it. I'm afraid you'll find the Heath very big—but I daresay you could search it in a day if you start at dawn. . . . I wish I could help you, but—ah! one thing I can do—I can send word to you if the Pumpkin appears anywhere in this neighbourhood while you are searching the Heath. . . ."

The Goblin's Heath

"That is very kind of you," said Molly. "It will help us a lot."

"And when you come to the village beyond—if you want to know of some one you can trust—go to Miss Marigold. Don't forget the name," said the Goblin.

"Miss Marigold," repeated Jack. "I'll remember. Thanks, very much."

"Do you know," smiled the Goblin, "when I heard that Old Nancy had sent the Pumpkin to the Impossible World, I thought it was a place like Dreamland—or a make-believe place, but now—if you say that you really are— I suppose you can't come down from the tree and let the other goblins see you?"

The children were about to reply, when a great hubbub and excitement arose among the goblins below, as a new goblin dashed in among them with some exciting news.

"Wait here," said the Goblin, "and I'll go and find what it's all about."

He soon climbed down and appeared among the crowd of eager, chattering goblins. Presently he slipped away again and scrambled up the tree to the children.

Knock Three Times!

"I'm glad you didn't come down," he said. "They are searching for you—the Pumpkin's spies are; an old woman and a young girl. Some of the goblins saw them about half an hour ago, on the main road over the Heath."

Jack and Molly began to shiver a little.

"It's all right," said the Goblin. "I haven't told the goblins where you are. I thought they'd be sure to want to see you, and this, of course, would attract attention. But I *have* told them to go and have some sport and to lead the old hag and the girl a real dance. I told them they were the Pumpkin's spies—they *will* lead them a dance too—making crackly noises in the bushes to lead them off the track — and running — and squealing — a regular goblins' dance we'll lead them. I'll go too and tell you what happens. I'll be back before dawn—this is my home, you know—this tree. Good-bye for the present," and he dashed away.

The children saw him swoop into a group of excited goblins and urge them to follow him—which they did. And presently there was scarcely a goblin in sight. They had all gone trooping away to the place on the Heath where the old woman and the girl were searching for Jack and Molly.

It seemed to the children that they waited in the tree for hours and hours, waiting, listening. Occasional sounds floated to them from the distance. They could hear squeaking and crackling, and once they heard a shrill scream. But they saw nothing, until the dawn broke.

Almost immediately afterward the Goblin returned, darting from out of the bushes opposite, popping into the hole in the tree trunk and scrambling up to them. In the pale glimmer of the morning light he told them what had happened, and how they had twice prevented the old woman from turning down the path that led past the children's hiding-place.

"They are gone from the Heath now," he said. "We drove them home, in the end, by darting out and pinching their legs and throwing prickly leaves at them. There were thousands of us goblins. . . . I wish you could have seen us. . . . When they found we were really in earnest and meant to get rid of them, and were not just teasing—they soon went. The old hag tried to tread on some of us—she was so angry; but we snatched her shoe off. and threw it into a pond."

"It's very kind of you to have helped us so," said Molly.

"We enjoyed it," said the Goblin. "It was great fun. And they really deserved it, you know."

And now that it was daybreak the Goblin bade good-bye to the children. "Remember," he said, "I will find some means of warning you throughout the day, if the Pumpkin is near." He popped down his hole; they heard him scramble a little way inside the tree—then all was quiet.

Jack and Molly looking out from the tree saw that all the other goblins had vanished. They waited a while until the day came, then they climbed down from their hiding-place, stretched themselves, and at once set about their search.

It was a difficult task, and a long one, for there seemed countless thick bushes, trees, hillocks, and winding paths on the Goblin's Heath. But they plodded on, searching eagerly and carefully. For a couple of hours they worked, then as the morning advanced they remembered that they had had nothing to eat since yesterday. So they climbed up another tree, so as not to be taken by surprise, and finished up the remains of Glan's 'snack,' while they discussed their plans for the day—studying their map so as not to leave any part of the Heath unsearched.

"There's one bit I'm afraid we must go back and do," said Molly, "though I don't like the idea of going near there again. You remember, Jack—we did not search the little bit of lane just beyond that—that house yesterday; that bit and the very beginning of the Heath."

They did not like the idea of going back to the Third Green Lane at all. But they went. When they came within sight of the lane they were amazed to find that the house had gone. It had vanished completely. Jack and Molly could scarcely believe their eyes at first, but on the whole they were distinctly relieved that it wasn't there; nevertheless, they searched the end of the lane and the edge of the Heath quickly, with constant, watchful eyes on the place where the house had been. Having satisfied themselves that the leaf was nowhere about there, they proceeded to the spot where they had left off searching, and continued peering among the bushes and trees and heather of the Goblin's Heath.

Knock Three Times!

Hour after hour passed by, and the day wore on. Still they plodded away at their task, keeping together and listening always, in case a message came from the Goblin. When they got hungry again, they ate some of Old Nancy's little brown sweets, and found them very refreshing.

In the daylight they could hardly imagine it was the same Heath that they had seen by moonlight; there was not the slightest trace of goblins, or spies. That is, not the slightest trace until they came across a pond and saw, half out of the water, and stuck in the soft mud, a shoe: a curiously shaped shoe, which they remembered, vaguely, seeing before—on the foot of the old woman with the horrible eyes. This was evidently the shoe that the goblins had thrown into the pond. The sight of it made all their recent adventures return vividly to their minds, and made them very unwilling to be still on the Heath when night came. So they hastened on their way.

Evening was already approaching when they finally came to the end of their day's search, and no sign of the Black Leaf had they found. As no warning had come from the Goblin and they had not been disturbed in any way, they felt, on the whole, all the better for their open-air day on the sunny, wind-swept Heath ; though they were tired now, and not at all sorry to turn their footsteps toward the little village, which appeared close at hand, at the edge of the Heath.

CHAPTER XIII

Timothy Gives Them a Clue

MISS MARIGOLD was in the garden tying up the sunflowers as Jack and Molly passed her cottage, which was the fourth one along the village street. Such a quaint little village street it was, with cobbled stones, and grass growing in the roadway, and bunchy white cottages with thatched roofs. The children did not know the name of the lady in the garden, of course, and were just wondering where Miss Marigold lived, when they saw a card hanging in the window, on which was printed :

> MISS MARIGOLD
> *Teas Provided.   Apartments.*

They stopped. Miss Marigold looked up from her flowers and saw two tired little faces looking at her over the gate. Miss Marigold was tall and thin and looked neither old nor young, but between the two. Her thick hair, which was of a pale yellow colour, was neatly braided round her head; she was dressed in a dark green dress with snow-white collar and cuffs. She looked kind when she smiled, and as she smiled when she saw the children they made up their minds to stay there if they could. So they opened the gate and entered her garden.

She listened while they told her who they were and what they wanted.

"I shall be pleased to give you accommodation," she said in her gentle, stiff little manner. "And you would like a cup of hot tea and some toasted muffins at once, I'm sure."

Jack and Molly felt that there was nothing they would like more than tea and muffins, but they told Miss Marigold that they had no money with them, and asked her what they could do for her to earn their tea, bed, and breakfast.

"Nothing at all. You are searching for the Black Leaf—that is enough. You will have done more for me, and for the whole country, than can ever be repaid, if you find it," said Miss Marigold, and led the way into her cottage, which was quaint

159

and old-fashioned, with low, oak-beamed ceilings and sloping floors.

The children had a refreshing wash, then sat down to a well-spread table—hot tea, and toasted muffins and eggs, and brown bread and butter, and honey, and fresh fruit. Over tea they told Miss Marigold about their search, and the latest doings of the Pumpkin. Miss Marigold had never actually seen the Pumpkin, but she had heard much about him, of course, and was very interested in the children's account.

"We have only just received news, in the village here, that the Pumpkin has returned. One of the villagers, who went to the city, came riding back over the Goblin's Heath with the news," she told the children.

While they were talking they heard footsteps on the garden path outside the window, and then came a tap at the door. Jack and Molly started. But Miss Marigold rose leisurely saying, with a shake of her head, "I told him not to stay as late as this." Then she opened the door. "Ah! come in, Timothy," she said.

Timothy came in. Catching sight of strangers

in the room, he paused, hesitating on the mat, nervously twisting his cap in his hands. Timothy was a fat, awkward-looking boy, about twelve years old, with puffy cheeks, and round eyes, and a simple expression. Miss Marigold introduced him as her nephew, much to the children's surprise, as he was utterly unlike his aunt in every way—in looks especially, except for the hair, which was the same pale yellow colour.

"Timothy has been out to a tea-party to-day," said Miss Marigold to the children. "Haven't you, Timothy?"

"Umth," lisped Timothy, in a thick voice, nodding his head.

"I hope you enjoyed yourself," said Molly, politely.

"Perapths," replied Timothy, sitting down on the extreme edge of a chair.

Molly looked puzzled, but he seemed well-meaning, and she felt sorry for him as he appeared to be so nervous.

"What kept you so late?" asked his aunt. "You ought to have been home an hour ago—you know I don't like you being out after dusk."

Knock Three Times!

Timothy blushed and began a jerky, stammering sort of explanation. His aunt frowned a little and looked at him suspiciously.

"You haven't been on the Goblin's Heath, have you?" Miss Marigold asked.

"No, ma'm," replied Timothy, promptly. "Where have you come from?" he asked Jack suddenly.

"We've just come from the Goblin's Heath," replied Jack; and at Timothy's eager request to be told about their adventures, Jack started to tell him about their search. Timothy appeared to listen intently, until presently his aunt got up and went out of the room to prepare the bedrooms. Immediately he leant across the table and interrupted.

"Here!" he exclaimed suddenly.

Jack stopped speaking, and stared at Timothy, who was obviously in a very excited state.

"Here, I thay! What do you thig?" said Timothy.

"What? What is it? What's the matter?" asked Jack.

"I theen *it*," said Timothy, and exploded with laughter.

Jack and Molly exchanged bewildered glances,
162

Timothy Gives Them a Clue

while Timothy rolled and rocked in his chair with laughter till the tears ran down his fat white cheeks. He continued to gasp and laugh until Molly grew quite concerned about him, and jumping off her chair she ran to the door to call his aunt. This sobered him immediately and he sprang up waving his hand to stop her.

"Don't, don't," he managed to gasp. "I alwayth laugh when . . . he! he! he! . . . when I exthited . . . don't call aunt . . . I tell you . . . he! he! he! he! . . . in a minute."

When he had quieted down a bit he said:

"Aunt muthn't know, becauth 'e thig I been out to tea—well, I haven't—and I been where 'e told me not to go, and I *theen* it!" He was getting fearfully excited again.

"Seen what? Oh, do tell us," said Molly.

"The . . . he! he! he! . . ." Timothy giggled. "The . . . Black Leaf!"

"Oh," cried Jack and Molly together, their questions tumbling over each other in their eagerness. "Where is it? Where did you see it? Did you pick it? What did you do with it?"

"I didn't pick it—I couldn't get near it," Timothy

answered. "But I know where it ith . . ." He leant toward them and whispered hoarsely, his eyes round and bulging. ". . . In the Orange Wood."

Timothy went on to tell them how he had happened to see it. It seemed that he had been forbidden by his aunt to go on to the Goblin's Heath, or into the Orange Wood, because it was rumoured that the Pumpkin's spies were in hiding in both these places—it was even said by some that the Pumpkin himself had been seen on the Heath yesterday. Although Timothy didn't believe this, he said, he longed to explore both the wood and the heath, and to-day he had deceived his aunt, pretending he was going to tea with a friend and instead had slipped into the wood, which lay just beyond the village, and had wandered about there. He had come across Mr Papingay's house in the wood—which he had often heard about, but never seen before. (Mr Papingay! Jack and Molly recognised the name, of course; it was Glan's relation.) He was a funny old man, was Mr Papingay, said Timothy; and it was a funny house. And the Black Leaf was growing in a plant-pot, in the house! Only don't tell his aunt he'd been in the wood, he pleaded, she would be angry with him, and perhaps send him away home to his father : and he didn't want to go home yet.

"Wait till you've got the Leaf—then it won't matter," said Timothy.

He seemed so distressed at the idea of his aunt knowing of his disobedience (although she didn seem the kind of aunt to be too severe, Molly thought) that the children promised they would say nothing about it.

"Couldn't you come with us, to-morrow, and show us the way ?" said Jack.

But Timothy shook his head. " I rather you tell me about it afterwarth," he said. " I had enough of the wood. Ith too full of crackly noith. I ran all the way home," he confessed. " Oh, and thereth one thig. Don't let Mr Papingay know you've come for the Leaf. He'th a funny old man, perapth he wouldn't let you have it. Wait till you thee it. It wath on the kitchen window thill—inthide—when I thaw it."

The children thanked Timothy, and were discussing eagerly to-morrow's plans, when Miss Marigold looked in to say all was ready upstairs.

"I heard you laughing a lot just now, Timothy,"

she remarked. " That tea-party made you very excited,
I'm afraid."

" Umth," agreed Timothy, meekly.

The children were very tired that night, and in
spite of their excitement they slept soundly in the
comfortable, warm beds Miss Marigold had prepared
for them.

Their first waking thoughts were of the plant-pot
in Mr Papingay's house : they longed to be off to
the Orange Wood without delay. But they discovered, on arriving downstairs, that the village had
made other plans for them. Somehow the news had
spread that two people from the Impossible World
had come to search the village for the Black Leaf,
and the villagers meant to welcome them handsomely
and give them all the help they could. During
breakfast the children noticed that people kept stop-
ping and peering in through the window at them, and
from remarks dropped by Miss Marigold they understood that they would create great disappointment,
if not give real offence, unless they searched the
village thoroughly that day—and in sight of the
people. Jack and Molly began to feel as if they
were a sort of show or entertainment. However, they

talked things over together, and calculating that the village ought not to take more than a few hours to do—as it was very small—they decided that perhaps they had better search it first, and then in the afternoon start off into the Orange Wood. After all Timothy might have made a mistake, and the Leaf might be in the village after all; it would never do to pass it by.

So they set to work immediately after breakfast, much refreshed by their long sleep and the wholesome, good food that Miss Marigold had set before them. They thanked her warmly and said good-bye to Timothy, then stepped out into another day of sunshine.

But they had reckoned their time without the villagers. So insistent and eager were they to help the children that they hindered and delayed them in every way. Children and men and women suggested likely places where the Black Leaf might be growing, and insisted on taking Jack and Molly to the places; but each search proved in vain.

They searched a field by special request of the man who owned it, and who expressed great surprise when told that the Leaf was not there. (Although

167

he knew very well that the Leaf was not there as he had already gone over the field himself. Still he felt he couldn't have his ground neglected when all his neighbours' fields were being searched.)

And one old lady insisted on digging up her window box to show them that the Leaf wasn't there, conscious of the importance she was gaining in the eyes of her neighbours while the children stayed about her place.

The attention they received made the children rather uncomfortable. However, every garden, every yard of roadway, every field and lane and paddock, and even every plant-pot, having been searched to the villagers' (and the children's) satisfaction, Jack and Molly at length said good-bye to the village and turned eagerly toward the Orange Wood.

The afternoon was well advanced by this time, and the sun gleaming through the trees in the wood turned the gold and brown leaves on the branches to a mass of flaming colour.

CHAPTER XIV

Mr Papingay's House in the Orange Wood

AS soon as the children entered the wood all sounds of life seemed to die away, and everything was still. No birds sang or fluttered overhead; no little wood animals scurried through the dry, dead leaves on the ground; no breeze rustled the golden leaves on the trees; the sun shone softly through the branches and cast a strange orange-coloured shimmer over the scene—which accounted for the name by which the wood was known. As Jack and Molly went along they found themselves talking to each other in whispers, afraid to disturb the brooding quietness of the wood; the sound of their footsteps on the path seemed unusually loud.

"I say, Molly, what do you say if we keep to the footpath and go straight to Mr Papingay's house as quickly as possible and see if it really is the Leaf?

169

Then we can search the rest of the wood afterward —if it isn't," suggested Jack.

Molly agreed readily. Remembering that it was rumoured that the wood was full of the Pumpkin's spies, the children had great hopes that it was the Black Leaf in Mr Papingay's plant-pot; for the spies would surely be stationed all around the place where the Black Leaf grew, to guard it.

"Thank goodness we know we can trust Mr Papingay," said Molly. "If we can only find him. Oh, Jack, if only it is the Leaf, won't it be splendid!" Molly broke off and glanced over her shoulder. "How awfully quiet everything is, Jack—just as if the wood were *listening!* . . . Oh! What was that!"

"It wasn't anything. Don't, Molly. You gave me quite a jump," Jack said unsteadily, looking over his shoulder too. The light in the wood was beginning to fade, and under the distant trees dim shadows gathered.

"I thought I heard some twigs crackling—a snapping sound," said Molly, wide-eyed.

"Well, you needn't say so, Moll, if you did. But anyway, I'm not afraid—if you are." Nevertheless

The House in the Orange Wood

Jack quickened his pace to a sharp trot, and Molly had some difficulty in keeping up with him.

" I'm not afraid, either," she gasped.

" Nor am I," repeated Jack, and went a little faster.

Then they both began to run.

"Of course—we ought—to—get there—as quick —as—we can—so—as not to—waste—any—time," Molly jerked out, apologizing as it were to herself and to Jack for their sudden haste.

They ran along the footpath for a short distance until, a little way ahead of them, they saw an open space in the wood, in the centre of which stood a house.

"Let's—stop—Molly," said Jack, breathlessly. They both pulled up and stood still for a few moments. "It wouldn't—do—for—us—to run in— on—on—him like this. It might look as if—as if we were—as if——oh, well, it would look funny, you know."

Molly agreed. So they waited until they had got their breath again, then they walked casually out into the open space. The trees stood round the clearing in a wide circle, and above the house was a big expanse of sky. It seemed quite light out here after the dim light of the wood.

It was a queer-looking house that faced them, but what it was about the house that made it queer Jack and Molly could not at first make out. Around it was a square of asphalt, and drawing nearer they saw that on the asphalt, all round the four sides, were rows of narrow white streaks, that looked like railings lying down flat; and this is what they actually proved to be—only they were not real railings, they were painted on the ground with white paint. The children looked up, and then they realized what it was that made the house look funny. Nearly everything on it and about it was *not real* but painted. The house itself was real, and so was the front door; but the knocker and handle and letter-box were all painted on. Three of the windows seemed real, but there were three more that were obviously painted on, and were obviously the work of some one not greatly skilled in the art of painting. There was a large tree painted on the asphalt, and a row of tulips, and a path bordered by painted stones that led up to the front door.

The children were gazing at these things in

The House in the Orange Wood

astonishment when the front door suddenly opened, and the owner of the house appeared on the threshold.

"Come inside," he called affably, peering at them over the top of his spectacles. "The latch on the gate pulls downward. Don't be afraid of the dog; he won't hurt you if I speak to him. There, Percy, there! Down, sir! There's a good dog!"

Jack and Molly looked round wonderingly, but could not see any signs of a dog, till their eyes caught sight of a black smudge of paint, which proved on closer acquaintance to be a black dog chained to a red kennel—both painted flat on the ground a few feet inside the gate. The children gazed at each other questioningly; then Glan's words came back to them, "Humour him, he's a queer old soul."

So Molly bent down and pretended to pull the latch on the gate down; she and Jack walked carefully on to the asphalt over the flat gate, then she turned and pretended to close and latch the gate again. As they passed the painted dog, she had another happy idea. "Good dog. Good dog," she said, and stooped and patted the asphalt.

Knock Three Times!

The old man beamed down upon her. "He's quite harmless when I tell him it's all right," he confided, "but you should just see him when he's roused. Stand on the step and I'll tell him there's a bath-chair round the corner. He hates 'em."

The children could not see a real step, but spying a painted white square by the front door, they stood on that.

"Now then," cried the old man, "at 'em, Percy, at 'em! There's a bath-chair a-comin' round the corner!"

There was a dead silence while the painted dog gazed with unseeing eyes up at the sky, and a little breeze rustled in the tree-tops.

"Isn't he furious?" chuckled the old man, beaming proudly from the dog to the children. "Go it, old boy! Give it 'em!"

As he seemed to expect an answer to his question, Molly said: "He—he—certainly looks very fierce, doesn't he?"

"That's nothing to what he can look," said Mr Papingay, obviously delighted at Molly's reply. "But, come inside, come inside."

So the children entered the narrow, dark hall

The House in the Orange Wood

and Mr Papingay shut the front door behind them.

"This way," he said, crushing past them and throwing open a door on the right. "Come inside and sit down a bit. This is my study. What do you think of it?"

As the question was asked before Jack and Molly were inside the room there was naturally a short interval before Molly could reply, politely:

"What a very—er—uncommon room."

"All done by myself," said the old man, waving his hand with a sweeping movement toward the walls.

The children followed the hand-sweep and saw rows upon rows of books painted round the walls. There was no doubt about them being painted. And they noticed also that the carpet, chairs, tables, curtains, and even the fireplace were all painted in this amazing room. Jack's eyes travelled rapidly over the room, but not a single real thing could he see in it except himself, and Molly, and the old man standing in front of him; and he looked at the latter twice to make sure that he was real and not simply made of paint like the other things. But Mr Papingay was real enough with his spectacles and bald head. The only hair he possessed grew like a fringe at the back of his head, low down, just above the nape of his neck—and under his chin a little fringe of whiskers appeared; he had round, blue eyes and eyebrows set high that gave him a look of continual surprise; over a dark-coloured suit he wore a brown plaid dressing-gown, with long cord and tassels, and on his feet were a pair of very old red felt carpet slippers. And then Jack's roving eye noticed that the buttons on his dressing-gown were painted on; but that was the only bit of paint about Mr Papingay.

"You see, it's so handy making my own things," he was explaining to Molly. "I can have any kind of things I like and change them as often as I like."

"Don't you find the chairs rather awkward to sit on?" inquired Jack.

"Not at all. Why should I?" replied the old man, slightly offended.

"Well—I—er—well, you see—they're not real, are they?" Jack blundered on.

"Not real! What do you mean?" snapped Mr Papingay. "Of course they're real. Sit on one and see."

The House in the Orange Wood

"Don't be silly, Jack," Molly broke in. "They certainly look most comfortable. I do think it is clever of you to make them," she said to the old man.

"Oh, no, no. Not at all. Simple enough," said Mr Papingay airily, appeased at once. "But you try one. They may look comfortable, but it's nothing to what they are to sit on. You try one," he urged.

So Molly pretended to sit down on one of the painted chairs. It was a most curious sensation. Although she knew there was no chair there she felt somehow as if she really were sitting on a chair; so that when the old man asked her, with a self-conscious smile on his face, "Now, isn't it comfortable?" she could answer truthfully, "Yes, it really is."

Yet, afterward, Jack told her that he had tried one of the chairs when she and the old man were not looking, and had nearly fallen on the floor. "I found it anything but comfortable—the silly old ass," he said.

When they had admired the study to the old man's content he led them out into the hall again and up the stairs to a curious little room he called his visitors room. As they went upstairs Molly tried to tell their host who they were and how they knew Glan and his father, but he kept up a constant stream of conversation himself and took no notice of her remarks.

The children found the visitors room more difficult than ever to be truthful and yet polite in. It had been hard to pretend the painted stair-carpet was soft and real, and that the books in the study could be taken out and read; but these things were nothing compared to the difficulties in the visitors room. It was a small, high-ceilinged room, furnished with painted chairs and tables; only, in addition to the painted furniture were painted people. Round the walls and on the floor, people standing, people sitting, ladies, gentlemen, girls and boys; some with hats on as if paying an afternoon call, some with hats off as if they had come to spend the day. But one and all, without exception, were simply painted people. On the panes of one of the real windows was painted the figure of a sandy-haired man, back view; this gentleman, who was dressed in a dull grey suit and a high white collar, was apparently looking out of the window.

As the children glanced round at these queer

The House in the Orange Wood

silent people, hesitating what to do, they became aware that the old man was murmuring some kind of introduction to a painted lady in bright purple.

"This is my dear friend, Mrs Pobjoy," he was saying. "Mrs Pobjoy, allow me to introduce you to my two little friends—er—what are your names, by the way?"

The children told him, and took this opportunity of explaining who they were and how they knew Glan.

"Dear me, dear me!" said Mr Papingay. "How very extraordinary!" and he shook hands affably, and then he introduced them to Mr Pobjoy—a red-faced gentleman painted on the wall beside his wife.

Molly bowed politely. "I'm very pleased to meet you," she said, and gave Jack a nudge with her elbow.

"Howjer do?" said Jack, feeling an awful ass.

The painted lady in bright purple stared vacantly down at the two children.

"Mrs Pobjoy's always delighted to see new faces, aren't you, ma'm? Ah, ha! A regular butterfly. A regular butterfly. What do you say, Pobjoy?"

and Mr Papingay gave the painted figure of Mr Pobjoy a dig in the ribs, then turned from one to the other of his painted visitors chattering and laughing, and shaking his head. "And here's little Maudie. Well, and how is Maudie to-day?" and he stooped and playfully flicked the cheeks of a fat-faced little girl with yellow hair and a pink frock who was leaning against a painted sideboard. "Here's a little girl to see you, Maudie. You'll like that, won't you?" He turned to the children. "I'm afraid she's rather peevish this evening. She is sometimes. It's best to take no notice—she'll come round presently. Here's Mr Waffer, here by the window—I won't introduce you to him just at present, he's probably just got an inspiration I should think, by the way he stands absorbed in the scenery outside. He's a poet, you know. . . . But come over here and let Lizzie and her sister see you." He bundled away across the room followed by the two children.

"I say, Molly," whispered Jack, "do you think we should see the front of Mr Waffer through the window if we went outside and looked up. I *would* like to see his face."

"Why?" asked Molly with interest.

The House in the Orange Wood

"Because I don't believe he has one. Do remind me to look as we go out," said Jack.

"This," the old man was saying as they came up to him, "is Lizzie and here's her sister. Very bright girls, both of them," he added in an undertone so that the green-frocked Lizzie should not hear. And so he moved on introducing them to one after the other, and it began to look as if he would never tear himself away from the visitors room. At length Molly told him that they would not be able to stay much longer as they wished to get out of the Orange Wood before darkness came down.

"Oh, you mustn't go yet," he protested. "I've got a lot more to show you yet. . . . Ah! and that reminds me. . . . But first you must come and see my kitchen arrangements; they are absolutely first-rate; and then I have something very exciting to tell you." He nodded his head mysteriously.

Jack and Molly exchanged significant glances. As they followed him downstairs it struck them that although he was introducing them to everything and everybody in his house, yet he had never troubled to introduce himself. He had forgotten about that. He led the way to the kitchen, and the children noticed, in passing, a servant carrying a tray, painted on the passage wall a few yards from the kitchen door. ("How tiresome it must be for her never to get any farther," thought Molly, but she didn't say anything.)

The kitchen was very like the other rooms, nearly all paint. It worried Molly a little to notice that the sink was painted on the wall, and she wondered however Mr Papingay managed to wash up the cups and saucers in the tin bowl that was painted inside the sink; especially as the taps and cups and saucers appeared to be real. But she was afraid to ask any questions in case it delayed the "exciting" news that they were longing to hear.

A quick glance at the kitchen window sill on entering the room showed them that there was no plant-pot there now. After Mr Papingay had taken them a tour of the kitchen and they had admired everything from the oven with the painted round of beef on the shelf to the painted egg-whisk hanging on the dresser, their host bade them be seated on a bench by the kitchen window—which happened to be a real bench, much to Jack's relief—and then he said:

182

The House in the Orange Wood

"There is something I think you ought to know." He shut the kitchen door carefully so that the servant painted in the passage should not hear, while the children's hearts began to beat rapidly. Mr Papingay came back and stood before them.

"The Grey Pumpkin has returned to this land," he said solemnly, then waited for the exclamations of amazement which did not come.

"Of course, we know," said Jack, after a short pause.

Mr Papingay looked both surprised and offended. "Why, how's this?" he asked.

And the children told him, and explained about the search they were making.

"Well, well, well," he said at length. "I've been searching for the Black Leaf too. I searched every inch of the Orange Wood thoroughly, directly I heard the Pumpkin was back again. *And*—this is what I really wanted to tell you—what do you think I did when I found that the Black Leaf wasn't anywhere in the wood?" he asked excitedly.

"What?" cried both children together.

"Painted a Black Leaf," he said triumphantly, beaming with joy. "And here it is."

Knock Three Times!

He opened a cupboard door behind him and disclosed a plant-pot (which was real) in which grew a black leaf (which was painted). In fact it was so entirely artificial that it wasn't even a real leaf coloured black: it was cut out of newspaper, and painted with a thick black paint.

Jack and Molly did not speak for a moment or two. They could not. They were so thoroughly disappointed. Had they wasted all this valuable time 'humouring' Mr Papingay for nothing more than this? They had hardly realized how high their hopes had been, until now, when they were flung to the ground. It was with an effort that Molly kept back her tears; as for Jack, he felt he would like to kick something.

Meanwhile, Mr Papingay was perplexed at their silence. He lifted the pot down and set it on the floor in front of the bench.

"Well, what do you think of it?" he asked.

"What are you going to do with it?" asked Jack.

"I will tell you," said Mr Papingay. "I have decided that you shall have the leaf and take it back to the City. I was wondering, only yesterday, whom

184

The House in the Orange Wood

I could send it by. It isn't time for my yearly visit to the City yet, and besides, Percy has rather a nasty little cough—I can't leave him till he's better, poor old chap."

"But it won't be—be the same as the real Black Leaf," said Jack.

"Why not? Why not?" asked the old man touchily.

"Well—it isn't magic, is it?" objected Jack. "It won't have any power over the Pumpkin."

"I won't guarantee that it isn't magic, though it may not have the same power over the Pumpkin," the old man admitted. "But what's the odds! They won't know—the people won't know—and anyway it's very handsome to look at—and just think of how surprised everybody will be. . . ."

The children could see that it was no use arguing the matter. Mr Papingay was beginning to look quite hurt and annoyed, and so to humour him and to save any further delay the children thanked him and said they would be pleased to take it with them. (They little guessed then how glad they would be later on that they had taken it with them.)

Knock Three Times!

"It's very clever of you to make it," said Molly.

Immediately Mr Papingay's ill-humour vanished, and he smiled down at the leaf in an affectionate manner.

"Oh, I don't know about being clever," he said. "Well—it's not a bad piece of work," he admitted modestly.

"Well now—I think we really must be going," said Molly, "or else it will be too dark in the wood for us to find our way. Shall we pick the leaf and take it with us, then?"

"It looks so well in the pot—I like it best in the pot—take the plant-pot, too," said Mr Papingay. "I shall be coming to the City in a few days and then you must tell me all about it—what the people said when they saw it and—I suppose you *are* going straight back to the City?" he inquired. "You won't want to bother to search for the other Black Leaf now, until you see what the people say to this one, I'm sure."

Self-centred Mr Papingay! He actually thought the children would be more anxious to hear what people said about his leaf, than to continue their search for the real Leaf. But the children were

186

The House in the Orange Wood

quite determined about continuing their work and at length made him understand that they must go on; but they were hoping, they said, to return to the City shortly when they would be very pleased to show his leaf. Mr Papingay cheered up a bit at this, and said they had better take it then, as they would be bound to reach the City before him. Then he asked them where they were going to search next.

"You needn't bother about this wood—I've searched it from end to end, thoroughly—as I told you. And besides," said Mr Papingay, "it isn't wise to linger in this wood just now. The Pumpkin has spies about all over the place. Of course, they never touch me—Percy wouldn't let them —but you two—! And I'm quite certain the Leaf isn't in this wood—or I'd have had it before now."

The children had not much faith in Mr Papingay's careful searching, but glancing through the window they saw that it was now getting too dark to search the wood that night. They had better get out of it as quickly as possible, even if they had to return and search it in the morning.

They became aware of Mr Papingay murmuring

something in the way of an apology for not asking them to stay over night there—but he was already overcrowded with visitors, the Pobjoys and others, he said. He knew of a nice little farmhouse outside the wood where they would be comfortable. The children were pleased to know of the farmhouse; not for worlds would they have spent a night in this silent wood. Mr Papingay was so careless, he would be sure to leave a window unfastened, and the Pumpkin's spies would creep out from the trees and get into the house. At least, this is what the children felt, but they thanked Mr Papingay and told him not to apologize at all as they really couldn't stay, but must go along.

"I'll tell you what, then," said Mr Papingay. "I'll just get my lantern and come along with you and show you the quickest way out of the wood to the farmhouse."

The children were much relieved at this, feeling that company and a light in the dusky wood before them was an unexpected blessing. After a great deal of fuss and bustle he found his lantern and escorted them through the front door—calling some final words of instruction to Percy (who remained gazing pensively up at the evening sky); they passed through the gate, or rather, stepped off the asphalt, and started out. Mr Papingay insisted on carrying his plant-pot and leaf until he should have to part with it at the end of the wood; so with this under his left arm, and his lantern swinging in his right hand he strode ahead of the children, crying cheerily:

"Come along, come along. I'll show you a short cut out of the wood. Ah! I'm glad I brought my lantern—it'll be dark enough in some parts of the wood."

The children followed, gazing with puzzled expressions at his lantern. Then they understood. There would be no light from it in the darkest parts of the wood, for it was only a painted lantern.

CHAPTER XV

Jack's Misfortune

THE children were obliged to walk quickly in order to keep pace with their guide, who trotted along rapidly, never troubling to glance round to see if they were coming. Once they had left the clearing and the queer little house behind them, and plunged into the wood, they found it quite dark; and darker still as they got farther in. Strange crackly noises could be heard from time to time behind the bushes and trees, which suggested all sorts of things to you if you happened to be a little girl or boy with a fairly active imagination.

Of course, there was always Old Nancy's gift— the matches—if the darkness grew unbearable. Both Jack and Molly remembered the matches, but they did not feel quite sure whether this was the proper time to use them, as they were afraid of offending their guide if they suggested that his lantern did not give enough light.

They trotted along in silence for a time, until a

particularly loud crack behind a bush close by startled Molly and made her feel that she could not bear the silence any longer.

"Don't you find it very lonely here—living by yourself in the wood?" she asked the hurrying figure in front of her.

"Eh?" asked Mr Papingay.

It was such a relief to talk that Molly gladly repeated her question.

"Not a bit of it," replied the old man, without slackening his pace or turning round. "Why should I? I have plenty of visitors—and Percy to take care of me."

"Yes, but aren't you afraid of—robbers—or anything?" asked Molly.

"Robbers!" the old man chuckled. "I should like to see the robber that could get past Percy. Besides, what is there to steal? That's the best of a house like mine, you see. No one can take things from me. I get all the use and pleasure I want out of the things I paint—then when I want new things I paint the old ones out and paint fresh ones in their place. And they can't be stolen—they're of no use to any one else, you see. As for the Pumpkin's spies," he continued in a loud voice, that made Jack and Molly shudder in case he were overheard. "I'm not afraid of them—they never touch me. . . ."

Molly gave a little scream, as something swept past her head, brushing her forehead as it did so.

"It's only a bat, Molly. Don't be a silly," said Jack in a shaky voice.

"There's heaps of them about—and owls," said Mr Papingay, continuing his rapid walk without a moment's pause. As if to confirm his words there came a mournful "Hoo, hoo, hoo," from the depths of the wood. The children gripped each other's arms tightly, and hastened on.

Another minute, and a patch of light appeared in the distance, and the children saw that it was the end of the wood.

"There," said the old man as they came out from the trees at last, "you can find your way now, can't you? I must get back—Percy doesn't like me to stay out very late. That is the farmhouse, over there; straight across this field, over the stile and the wooden bridge across the river, and a few minutes' walk up the hill, on the other side. You can see where I mean, can't you?" And he pointed the farm out to the children. "You can mention my name to them—Farmer Rose knows me well. Now if you will take this," he said, passing the plant-pot containing his precious leaf into Molly's keeping. "And take care of it. I shall see you both again shortly, I hope. Good-bye. Good-bye."

"Thank you so much for bringing us this short cut out of the wood," said Molly. "It was awfully kind of you."

"Rather," said Jack. Then, relieved at being safely out of the wood, he added generously, "I say—your lantern's a marvel!"

The old man nodded and beamed delightedly. Then, waving his hand, he stepped back into the wood, his painted lantern swinging at his side, and disappeared.

As soon as Mr Papingay had gone, Jack and Molly stopped and looked around them. They were in the open country once more, but a more hilly country than that on the other side of the wood, for they had passed right through the wood and come out at the opposite end.

The wood led straight out into a field, across which a narrow footpath straggled to a stile set in the middle of green hedges. On the other side of the stile was a path, and a little white wooden bridge across the river, and on the farther side of the river were hills and the farm-house. The red roofs and whitewashed walls of several cottages and other farm-houses could be seen here and there.

Evening was closing in rapidly, and while they had been in the wood dark clouds had drifted up and were now gathering threateningly overhead.

" It's too dark to do any more searching to-night," said Jack. " I suppose we'd better make straight for the farm ; and come back and search all round here in the morning."

" I suppose that would be best," said Molly. " I don't feel at all satisfied about the Orange Wood, do you, Jack ? I think we must come back and search that too—to-morrow. It doesn't look a very big wood."

As the children turned to look back at the wood, the first spots of rain began to come down, so they hastened along the path toward the stile.

" I wonder if Mr Papingay really has searched it thoroughly," said Molly. " He seems such a funny old man—I don't know what to think."

Jack's Misfortune

"I do," laughed Jack. "Mr Papingay's much too slap-dash to search it carefully. No, Moll, I'm afraid we've got to do it to-morrow. It won't be so bad in daylight. My word! How the rain is coming down. We're in for a storm, I should think."

They hurried on, climbed the stile, but when they got on to the bridge Molly stopped for a moment.

"I say, Jack," she called, and Jack stopped too. "I'm going to throw this plant-pot in the river—it's too heavy to take all the way with us, and I don't like to put it down in the field in case Mr Papingay comes along and finds it." She pulled the leaf out of the pot, folded it up, and pushed it into her satchel, then threw the pot into the swiftly flowing river.

"What are you keeping the leaf for?" cried Jack. He had to raise his voice to be heard through the rising gale.

"Oh, I couldn't throw that away," said Molly. "And besides, it may come in useful," she added as she ran along beside Jack up the hill. "You never know."

"Won't old Timothy feel sold when he hears what his Black Leaf really was!" chuckled Jack.

The rain was coming down heavily as they reached

the front door of the farm-house. They knocked, and rang at the bell—but no one answered, and there was no sound within the house. They knocked again, then went round and knocked at the back door. But still no one came, and they began to fear that there was nobody at home. This proved to be the case. The stables and outhouses were all locked up, although they could hear a horse inside one of the buildings, and there were some fowls in a hen-run in the yard. Evidently the people were only out for a short time, so Jack and Molly decided to take shelter in the porch by the front door for a while, until the storm was over, or Farmer Rose returned.

"Oh, dear, what a dreadful night it's going to be!" said Molly. "Are you very wet, Jack?"

"Hardly a bit. It's quite comfortable in this porch," Jack replied, and then she heard him chuckling. "I was just thinking of old Mr Papingay," he explained, and then he broke off with a sudden exclamation: "Oh, bother!"

"What is it?" Molly asked.

"I clean forgot to look for Mr Waffer's face! Why didn't you remind me?" said Jack.

Jack's Misfortune

"I forgot too," answered Molly. "Never mind, we'll look to-morrow if we search the Orange Wood."

"We mustn't let Mr Papingay see us, though. What fun! It'll be like playing hide-and-seek," said Jack. "Goodness, how the wind *is* howling!"

They remained quiet for a time, huddled up in the porch. The storm was growing still worse, and it was very dark now. Presently the silence in the porch was broken by Jack exclaiming again: "Bother!"

"What is it now?" inquired Molly.

"Oh, I say, Moll—I've lost them—yes, I've lost my box of matches—Old Nancy's matches."

A thorough search of Jack's satchel and all his pockets proved that this was unfortunately true.

"They must have fallen out—let me see now—I had them just before we climbed the stile, I'm sure of that, because I put my hand in my satchel to get one of those sweet squares and I remember feeling the box." Jack tried hard to think back. "I believe I must have dropped them somewhere just by the bridge. Here, Molly, hold my satchel and things a sec, will you, and I'll just run down to the bridge and fetch the box—yes, I'm sure now I heard something

197

fall on the bridge. I won't be a couple of minutes. You wait here, Molly; I'll be ever so quick. No, it isn't raining much."

"Don't go, Jack!" cried Molly. "It's so dark and wet, oh, Jack, don't go! I've still got my matches left —never mind yours now."

But Jack was hardly listening. "It's only just down the hill—won't be a minute—you wait here—I must get them, Molly—we may need them. It isn't so dark—I can see all right."

"Wait, wait, Jack. Oh, I know—let me strike one of my matches and see if it can find the other box for us." Molly was fumbling in her satchel quickly. But Jack hadn't heard her, and had started off impetuously, calling back, "Shall be back in a minute. Wait there, Moll."

"I'm coming too," called Molly, but the wind howled past and Jack did not hear as he raced down the hill.

Fastening up Jack's satchel and slipping it over her shoulders together with her own satchel, and clasping her own box of matches firmly in her hand, Molly set out after her brother, calling his name as she ran. It was very silly of Jack to tear off like this, she thought, but she was only anxious to get him back safely in the porch again out of the darkness and the rain. She did not stop to light one of her matches until she was about half-way down the hill. Then she stopped and struck one. No ordinary match would have kept alight a second in such a storm, but Old Nancy's matches, as she already knew, were not ordinary. The light gathered all on one side as usual, pointing straight down the hill.

Molly had just time to see the figure of Jack running in front of her—he had reached the bridge— when the match flame veered right round and pointed up the hill.

Molly turned and looked, but there was nothing to be seen there. What did it mean? She hastened on down the hill, and as her match went out, she lit another one.

This time the light from the match showed her that Jack was on the bridge and had crossed over to the footpath, and was bending down to pick something up. So he had found his matches! But even as she saw Jack, her eye caught sight of something coming from the direction of the Orange Wood along the river bank, toward the bridge. Then the flame from the match veered round and pointed up the hill. But not before Molly had seen what it was that was creeping toward Jack on the other side of the river.

It was the Grey Pumpkin. And Jack had not seen him.

And the match flame was pointing the way of escape, up the hill to safety! Just as the flame had pointed out the way of escape in the underground cellar.

But there was no thought of her own safety while Jack was in such danger. Molly dashed forward, crying out: "Jack! Run! Quick! Come back! Look behind you!" But the wind roared around her as if mocking her, and Jack never heard.

As she ran she lit another match, and by its light saw that Jack was standing upright and had turned —and seen the Pumpkin close behind him. He went to run, but slipped and fell to his knees, and as he was scrambling up again the Pumpkin reached him. Jack seemed to collapse all in a heap on the ground, and then, there was no Jack—but in his place another great Grey Pumpkin. Molly pulled up and stood motionless, gazing with horrified eyes. Then her match went out. She lit another mechanically, and

as she did so she heard a terrific crash a few yards
ahead, and saw that the storm had broken down
the wooden bridge; it collapsed into the river and
was caught up by the rapidly rushing current and
swirled away. If this hadn't happened, Molly would
have been over the bridge in another second (forgetting in her despair that she could do no good and
would only get caught herself). But as it was, she
was brought to an abrupt standstill at the water's
edge, while on the other side of the river two Grey
Pumpkins rolled slowly away along the path toward
a group of tall dark trees. . . .

And so it was that the farmer and his kindly wife,
returning home about half an hour later, found a little
girl sitting in the porch by their front door, crying as
if her heart would break.

CHAPTER XVI

Molly Accepts a Present

THE farmer's wife proved a friend indeed to Molly. She gathered the little girl up in her arms and carried her indoors, made her put on some fresh clothes while she dried her wet things before a blazing fire, and not until Molly had emptied a big bowl of hot bread and milk would she let her say a word of thanks or explanation.

Then, when the farmer and Mrs Rose and Molly (wrapped in a warm cloak belonging to the farmer's wife) sat round the fire, Molly told them her story, weeping afresh at the memory of Jack's misfortune.

"There, there, my dear," comforted Mrs Rose, her own eyes full of tears. "It's no use crying, you know. What you have got to do is to determine to find the Black Leaf, and then, like as not, you'll get your brother back again."

"Oh, I *am* determined to find it," cried Molly. "I was determined before—but I will—I *will* find it—whatever happens."

Molly Accepts a Present

"You must try to get a good rest to-night, and then you can start off fresh in the morning—and you mustn't cry any more or you'll make yourself ill—and then you won't be able to do anything," said Mrs Rose.

Molly quite saw the wisdom of Mrs Rose's words and tried her best to stop crying. But she kept thinking about Jack, and wondering what they were doing to him, and why the Pumpkin had changed him into a likeness of himself. Supposing she had to return home to Mother without Jack. She couldn't. She wouldn't, she vowed to herself. She would stay in this country and search and search until the Black Leaf *was* found, even if she had to wait for years . . . and here her tears began to flow again.

To distract her, the farmer began talking about the country around and the most likely places to search. He had searched all his own land, he said, directly he heard the Pumpkin was back, and he had helped to prepare some of the beacons on the hills around this district. And he asked Molly if she knew on which hills the beacons were set.

Molly dried her eyes, got her map out, and

showed him how the beacon hills were marked, and soon she and the farmer and Mrs Rose were poring over the map, planning out the best routes to take, and discussing the most likely places for search. The farmer showed her all the places where the Leaf was *not* growing, places he had personally searched; and at Molly's request he marked these places on the map with a lead pencil. Molly decided to herself that she would leave these marked places until the very last, until she had searched all the more likely parts round about. She felt she could not leave them out altogether, although she trusted the farmer absolutely; she had promised to search each part herself.

When she mentioned Mr Papingay's name the farmer and his wife smiled, and although they thought he would certainly have searched the Orange Wood as he said he had, yet he was not sure to have done it thoroughly, and they agreed with Molly that it would be as well to go over the ground again if possible. The fact that the Pumpkin was lurking about there made all three of them think that probably the Leaf was growing somewhere near. Of course, this might not be so; it might be only the

Molly Accepts a Present

Pumpkin's object to prevent Jack and Molly going any further with the search.

"You'll have to be very cautious, missie, if you go back to the wood," said Farmer Rose. "It wouldn't do for you to get caught too."

"I'll be very careful—but it won't do for me to be afraid, or p'r'aps I'll never get Jack back again," said Molly. "I mustn't be afraid of anything now."

"That's the spirit," said the farmer, slapping his knee. "And if there's anything we can do to help you—you've only got to name it—we shall be proud."

When the farmer's wife tucked her up in bed, about twenty minutes later, Molly threw her arms round her neck.

"I don't know why you are so good to me," she said. "Thank you so much. I've given you a lot of trouble, I'm afraid."

"Not the least bit in the world," replied the farmer's wife. "Try to get to sleep, my dear. . . . P'r'aps to-morrow—who knows what may happen to-morrow!"

Molly was so exhausted that she slept soundly

and dreamlessly, in spite of the fact that the wind rattled furiously at her window and roared down the chimney. In the morning she woke with a dreadful, leaden feeling at her heart, but she determined not to brood over yesterday, but to get to work at once.

After breakfast she collected up all the things from Jack's satchel and put them with her belongings into her own satchel. The farmer's wife insisted on giving her a big packet of food for luncheon, and told her to come back and sleep at the farm again that night if she ended her day's search anywhere near.

Molly thanked her gratefully, then started out alone. The rain had ceased, and the wind was much less violent, but it was a grey day with a sky full of scurrying clouds.

And now began a long, wearying time for Molly. Alone, of course, the task of searching was longer and more difficult, though the enthusiasm with which she went to work kept her from realizing this to the full. She went on her way searching eagerly and thoroughly that part of the valley through which the river ran, which came within her square of map; she crossed the water by another bridge about a mile away from the place of last night's accident, and searched the opposite bank, gradually working her way back to the spot where the Pumpkin had appeared.

Across the water she could see the farm-house, half-way up the hilly road on the other side. Behind her was the stile which she and Jack had clambered over yesterday. Was it only yesterday?—it seemed more like a week ago to Molly. She climbed over the stile again and crossed the field, searching as she went, to the Orange Wood.

Very cautiously she entered the wood, and started her search, ears and eyes constantly on the alert, and hands and feet ready to spring and climb up a tree at any moment, if the need arose. But the need did not arise, and presently Molly found she was back within sight of Mr Papingay's house. She went extra carefully now, so as not to attract the old man's attention, and made a tour of the wood near his house, working in a wide circle, so as not to cross the space before his front door. Once she heard his voice calling out to know what Percy was barking at, but she did not see him.

And though at length she searched the whole of the Orange Wood, she did not find the Black Leaf; nor did she see any sign of the Pumpkin or his spies.

So she left the wood behind her, and came back over the river, and made her way to the farm-house again, where she had tea, and told them all about her day's search. But she would not stay the night there, as there was still a long light evening to work through, and she hoped to get some way on the road to Lake Desolate before the night fell.

"You'll pass several houses and cottages on the road," said Mrs Rose, and proceeded to give Molly the names of several friends of hers, whom she could trust. "But be sure to come back here, if you want to."

Mrs Rose stood at the gate waving her handkerchief to Molly, until the little girl turned round a bend in the road and was lost to sight. Then she dabbed her eyes with the handkerchief. "Bless the child," she said, as she hurried indoors. "She deserves to win."

208

Molly Accepts a Present

From the top of one of the hills close by, Molly found she could get a splendid view of the surrounding country. The clouds had disappeared by now, and it promised to be a beautiful evening and a moonlight night. The river sparkled beneath, and the Orange Wood glowed in the evening sun, while far away, in the distance, she could see the white towers of the City. Looking down at the Orange Wood she suddenly remembered that she had forgotten to look for Mr Waffer's face, as she passed Mr Papingay's house. What a pity! Jack would have liked to know, when—when she met him again. But she had had so many things to think about in the wood that it is no wonder she forgot about Mr Waffer.

Descending the hill, Molly started on the road to Lake Desolate. It was pretty and green at first with cottages dotted about in small clusters, and presently she passed through a tiny village, where she stopped to inquire and search. But although every one seemed kind, and eager to help, there was nothing to be heard or seen of the Black Leaf.

About half a mile outside the village, Molly came to a few more houses and a small shop.

Knock Three Times!

At the door of the shop stood an old gentleman wearing a black skull-cap and a long, shabby coat. When he saw Molly approaching he came out to meet her and, seizing her hand, shook it warmly, saying that he had heard of her goodness in helping with the search and thanked her gratefully.

" I have been keeping a watch on the road for the last few days, missie, hoping to catch a glimpse of you as you passed," he said. " I heard you were coming this way."

Molly was pleased at his impulsive friendliness, especially as she was feeling very lonely just now. She stopped chatting for a few minutes, and the old gentleman proudly showed her his shop. He was a watchmaker, and the shop was full of watches and clocks of all kinds and sizes. Besides these, he had a small collection of jewellery.

" I expect you wonder at a watchmaker being right out here," he said, noting Molly's surprised expression at the contents of his shop. " Many people wonder at first. But I supply the clocks and watches for all the neighbouring towns and villages and even for the City. I send to the City twice a week. I live out here simply because my father and

Molly Accepts a Present

grandfather and great-grandfather have always lived in this place—and because my health won't permit me to live in crowded towns. . . . Now, miss, if you will be so good I want you to accept a little present from me, as a token of appreciation of the work you are doing."

He opened a little box and drew out a dainty, silver bracelet, that jingled as he handled it—just the very kind of bracelet that Molly had longed for on her birthday.

Molly's face lit up, but she hesitated. Ought she to accept this present from a stranger—especially as she had made up her mind not to trust anybody now, unless she was perfectly sure they were all right. The old watchmaker seemed harmless enough, and he was already looking disappointed at her hesitation. Molly felt it would be unkind to refuse the bracelet, and difficult also. It was not as if he had offered her food or drink, that might be poisoned ; nor had he made any effort to entice her into his shop; she had merely stepped inside on the mat and the door had been left wide open. Surely there could be no harm in accepting the bracelet, Molly argued to herself. It was so pretty, and she *would* like to have it, and anyway, if she felt doubtful afterward she could always get rid of it somehow, when the old gentleman could not see her and be hurt.

"I beg you will accept this bracelet," said the watchmaker. "I have been keeping it back specially for you."

So Molly accepted the bracelet, and the old gentleman 'had the honour,' as he put it, of seeing her slip it over her right hand, where it gleamed and jingled, and nearly slipped off when she put her arm down straight—just as she had longed for it to do. Molly thanked the old watchmaker and shook hands with him again, as she bid him good-bye.

He stood at his door bowing as Molly went on her way, but no sooner was she out of sight than he returned to his shop and, closing the door, sat down on a stool behind the counter, and began to shake with silent laughter; he continued to laugh, hugging himself while he did so, and rocking backward and forward, and bending himself nearly double, and all this quite noiselessly—the only sounds in the shop being the rapid tick, tick, tick, and the steady tick-tock, of the watches and clocks around him.

CHAPTER XVII

A Warning

MEANWHILE, after walking along for a short distance, Molly thought it would be wise to look up the names of Mrs Rose's friends, as the daylight was beginning to fade and already the moon was mounting the sky; she had scribbled the names and addresses down on a slip of paper. She noted, with a slight thrill of pleasure, the jingle of the silver bracelet as she took the paper out of her pocket. Poor Molly, she could not feel very happy about the bracelet, of course, as the weight of Jack's misfortune still crushed her down; but she was certainly pleased to possess such a bracelet. Having discovered that one of Mrs Rose's friends lived about a quarter of a mile farther on, she determined to search the road until she came to this house, and then ask if Mrs Jennet, for that was the friend's name, would kindly put her up for the night.

The road now began to grow wilder and more

rugged, while here and there, beside the way, were huge rocks and piles of stones. She passed an occasional tree, but these had few leaves on their branches, and were much twisted and bent as though lashed by many storms.

Molly continued to search, but, instead of hurrying along as she had meant to, she found herself moving slower, and gradually slower still, and became aware that she was suddenly very tired. She dragged on for a short distance.

"I can't do any more searching to-night," she thought to herself. "I'm too tired. I'll just make straight for the house—only I wish it wasn't such a long way off. I'll never get there."

Molly found great difficulty in keeping her eyes open now; and if she hadn't been so thoroughly exhausted and tired she might have been suspicious of this overwhelming wave of sleep that had seized her. She was too tired to think or reason, too tired to be suspicious. She only knew that her feet felt as if they were made of lead, and the only thing she wanted to do was to lie down and go to sleep at once.

"Can't reach the house," she murmured, drowsily. "Must go to sleep."

A Warning

She stumbled across the road, and threw herself down on the grass by the wayside. Oh, how delicious it was, just to lie down and go to sleep! But as her head was sinking back a last wave of consciousness flashed through Molly's mind of the foolishness of the thing that she was doing . . . going to sleep by the roadside . . . and if the Pumpkin came along . . . she would never be able to save Jack now. At this thought—she rallied for a moment and pulled herself up into a kneeling position. She remained thus for a moment or two, with her head drooping forward. Then she struggled to fight off the wave of sleep that was coming over her again, and managed to crawl a few paces further on.

Although Molly did not know it at the time, this was one of the most critical moments in her adventure. If she had given in and gone comfortably to sleep by the roadside, this story would have had a very different ending. But Molly did not give in, her desire to find the Black Leaf and save her brother was so strong, that in spite of the great odds against her she was able to make one last effort to reach a place of safety. Though there was still no sign of Mrs Jennet's house, there was fortunately a tree close by. And it was toward this tree that Molly slowly groped her way. She never knew how long it took her to reach that tree, although it was standing only a few feet away from her. But with repeated efforts she at length reached it, and with a great struggle pulled herself up into a standing position, leaning against the trunk. For some time she stood leaning against the tree; she could not remember afterward whether she went to sleep for a. while or not—she thought she must have gone to sleep (" Like a horse, standing up," she told herself). But she had barely lost consciousness when again her desire urged her to make another effort.

This was the last effort, and the hardest of all. Molly scarcely knew how she managed it, but manage she did, to pull herself up into the tree, and curl up among the lower branches. Then, immediately, she was asleep.

All through the moonlit night she slept and did not move. And if anyone passed on the road beneath the tree that night—Molly never knew. And nobody guessed there was a little girl lying asleep in the gnarled old tree by the side of the road that led to Lake Desolate. For little girls who are as tired as

A Warning

Molly must have been have not usually the strength, nor the will, to climb trees.

At daybreak Molly stirred and threw out her right arm, so that it hung down a little, over the edge of one of the branches: and the bracelet, the jingly, silver bracelet, slipped down over her wrist, and as she moved again, it slid over her hand and fell on to the ground at the foot of the tree.

After this Molly seemed more restless, and did not sleep so soundly, though many hours went by, and it was nearly noon before she was aroused at length by some one exclaiming loudly and persistently from beneath the tree, and something cold and hard grabbing at her arms and legs.

Molly sat up, rubbing her eyes, and then became aware that a chubby, startled-looking little woman in a black and white check dress and a black bonnet was calling up to her while she made frantic efforts to catch hold of Molly with the crooked handle of her umbrella.

"Oh, thank goodness, you 'ave woke up, which I thought you never was going to!" cried the plump little woman, dabbing her face with her handkerchief. "Such a fright as you give me, lying quite still there and me a-hollering at you for a hour or more, though I'd never a-seen you if it hadn't been for your 'and and arm 'anging down out of the tree. . . ."

"Who are you?" asked Molly drowsily. "I'm glad you did wake me up."

"Maria Jennet is my name," was the answer. "I done my best to wake you up, but my! you do want a bit of waking. Made me quite 'ot, you 'ave."

"Oh, are you Mrs Jennet?" said Molly. "Mrs Rose's friend?"

"I am," said Mrs Jennet emphatically.

"Why, I was on my way to your house last night, when—when . . . Oh!" Molly gave a scream.

"Oh!" screamed Mrs Jennet. "What is it now? You do give a body the jumps, you do!"

But Molly did not answer. She was gazing with horrified eyes at her right arm. On the wrist was a long grey stain!

How had it come there? What did it mean? Molly rubbed her arm vigorously with her pocket-handkerchief—but she could not remove the stain. She had seen a grey stain like this before; but where? . . . And then she remembered. It was on

218

A Warning

Old Nancy's finger, the evening she slept through the sunset hour. Molly then realized what had happened.

"Of course, he was another of them. What a stupid girl I was to trust him," she exclaimed. "But where has my bracelet gone! Wait a minute please," she continued, in reply to Mrs Jennet's excited questioning. "I'll tell you all about it in a minute." She climbed down from the tree and searched about in the grass beneath. "Ah, here it is!" she cried, and snatched up her bracelet, only to drop it again instantly, as if it were red-hot coals. For on the inner side of the bracelet she saw the remains of a dull grey powder still clinging to it. "So that's how he did it!" Molly nodded to herself. "That explains things."

She understood now that the watchmaker was another spy employed by the Pumpkin, and the bracelet which she had accepted from him had contained this magic powder which had rubbed off on to her arm, and sent her to sleep. The old watchmaker was evidently relying on the powder acting quickly, and Molly, overwhelmed by sleep, being compelled to rest by the side of the road — or somewhere where the Pumpkin could easily catch her. Luckily for Molly, she had had enough will power to fight her way to a place of safety; and luckily, also, the bracelet had slipped off and so gradually she had regained consciousness again. Molly had had a very narrow escape, and she felt decidedly bewildered as to the best way of winning through the difficulties around her. Of one thing she felt certain, she must be very distrustful of everything and everybody—except, of course, where people were recommended to her by some one she could trust. So far, all the links in her chain of friends had proved good and true; Glan—Old Nancy—Aunt Janet—The Goblin—Miss Marigold—Mr Papingay—Mrs Rose—and now, Mrs Jennet. She could trust Mrs Jennet, surely.

Mrs Jennet was bubbling over with curiosity about the stain and the bracelet, and Molly answering some of her numerous questions, asked her to lend her the umbrella for a minute. Mrs Jennet watched breathlessly while Molly dug a little hole with the point, then picked up the bracelet on the tip of the umbrella and dropped it in the hole and piled earth and stones on it.

A Warning

"It might only bring trouble to some one else if I leave it here," she said.

Then she accepted Mrs Jennet's kind and vigorous invitation to go home with her and 'have a bite of something' before proceeding on her way. As they walked along Molly told her companion a little of what had already taken place, and what had happened to Jack. At which Mrs Jennet protested loudly and even wept a little; then stood still in the middle of the roadway while she told Molly all the horrible things she would like to do to the Pumpkin if she caught him.

Mrs Jennet's house was only a short distance away, and stood with several other houses by the side of the main road—the last dwellings these before you reached Lake Desolate, which was about two miles further on, she told Molly. Molly learned that the men from these houses worked in the mines near by. Mrs Jennet's husband worked there and would not be home till evening.

While Mrs Jennet was bustling about, laying the table, and frying eggs and bacon, Molly got out her map and looked to see where the mines were. They were not marked on her map at all, and Mrs

Knock Three Times!

Jennet explained, when Molly showed her the map, that the mines were just over the border of Molly's square; at which Molly was rather relieved, as it had struck her that she might have to go down the mines perhaps to search for the Black Leaf. But on second thoughts she remembered—of course, the Black Leaf could only grow above ground. This incident, however, called Molly's attention to the fact that she was nearing another border-line of her square. It stretched away to the left of the road she was soon to go along; so she would not have much country to search on that side. But there was still a large piece of country around Lake Desolate.

"Are there no more houses beyond this group?" Molly asked Mrs Jennet, as they sat down to their meal.

"No. Yes," said Mrs Jennet. "That is, not until you've passed Lake Desolate. Then there are one or two sheep-farms and cottages on the 'ills. Very lonely they must be, too. There's very few go to Lake Desolate now—the road's so bad—and so lonely. And what's the good of going there, there's nothing to see but the Lake and the 'ills. . . . 'Ave

A Warning

some more bread, duckie. . . . And there's all them wild birds screeching over the Lake. Ugh! Fair gives me the creeps, it does. But there— I forgot you was going there. Fancy, a bit of a girl like you! Well, well! P'r'aps you ain't afraid of being alone though? Eh?"

Molly said she didn't think she was.

"I'm fond of my own company when I'm with other people," remarked Mrs Jennet. "You know what I mean—I feel a little bit lost by myself."

Everything in Mrs Jennet's room seemed like herself—plain and plump and loud, but nevertheless good-natured. The chubby-looking horse-hair sofa with the round large-patterned cushions reminded Molly strangely of its owner; and so did the round-backed chairs with their thick arms; even the carpet was just like Mrs Jennet would have looked if she had been a carpet. Molly began to wonder what Mr Jennet was like.

"I've got a photo of 'im—up there on the mantel-shelf—I'll show you," said Mrs Jennet in reply to a question from Molly.

But even as Mrs Jennet handed the photo down, Molly felt she knew what he would be like. And she was right. He was exactly like Mrs Jennet would have been if she had been a man.

"He's a dear old lad," said Mrs Jennet, eyeing the photo affectionately. "I wish you could have waited to see 'im—but if you do find the old Black Leaf 'e'll get a 'oliday I expect—every one will. My! Won't there be celebrations! And we'll all come down to the City and see you! 'Ave some more milk, duckie?"

Mrs Jennet chattered gaily on, asking and answering numberless questions. Molly asked her if she could tell her of any one she could trust, who lived in the little cottages or farms beyond Lake Desolate.

"Yes, yes. There's a very nice lady I know lives in one of them—in a little cottage on the side of the Giant's 'Ead—that's the name of the 'ill—it's shaped on top like a nuge 'ead. She's got a sweet, pretty cottage—stays there for 'er 'ealth. She's away sometimes staying with 'er sister in the City, but I should think she'd be 'ome this time of year. 'Er name's Lydia North—Miss Lydia we always call 'er. 'Ere, I've got a photo of 'er in my album. I'll show you. She very kindly give me one when she knew I collected photos, bless 'er 'eart!" said Mrs Jennet.

A Warning

The photo was of a refined, sweet-faced lady. Molly studied it intently so that she would know Miss Lydia when she saw her.

"Thank you very much," said Molly. "This will be a great help to me. I know one person I can trust anyway."

But Molly was not to get away as easily as that. Once Mrs Jennet had got her beloved album open she insisted on showing Molly all the photos of her relatives and friends, including Mrs Rose and Farmer Rose.

"I wish you had a photo of yourself about you," said Mrs Jennet. "I'd like you in the album."

Molly was sorry she couldn't oblige her hostess, but admired the collection of photographs with such enthusiasm that Mrs Jennet was enraptured. At length Molly managed to tear herself away, and bidding good-bye to Mrs Jennet, and thanking her warmly for all her kindness, Molly started out once more.

It was now early afternoon. Searching carefully along the road and on either side of it she proceeded slowly. As she went on, the country grew wilder and lonelier. The hills rose up on every side,

225

bare, gaunt hills on which nothing seemed to grow, and at the foot of the hills great rocks and stones were strewn. Molly soon left all signs of the miners' houses behind her, and as she looked back and could see nothing but the wild scenery all around her—no smoke from a chimney, no sign of human beings at all—she began to feel very small and lost and lonely. But she was not afraid. She realized, after thinking things over, that in the ordinary way the Pumpkin's spies could not touch her or make her do things by force; it had to be some carelessness or weakness in herself which enabled them to obtain a power over her. She would be very careful in future, and would not trust any one but those people who she *knew* were her friends. She would be on her guard all the time.

She searched carefully for about an hour, in every likely place along the way, keeping her eyes and ears constantly on the alert. And presently the latter informed her of the galloping of horse's hoofs in the distance. Looking back along the road she saw a cloud of dust, and by and by a big black horse, on which was seated a man in a slouch

A Warning

hat and flying cape, became visible. Molly glanced round for a place of escape, if necessary, or a place to hide; but there was no place to hide in this barren spot, and no trees near by. So she walked steadily on. So long as it wasn't the Pumpkin, the man on the horse could not touch her against her will—that is, if he was an enemy. Poor Molly expected every stranger to be an enemy now, of course. Maybe the horse and rider had no business with her at all. Anyway, they came dashing along at full speed, thundering on the road behind her.

Molly drew to the side of the road to let them pass. But they did not pass. She heard, with a sinking heart, the horse gradually slacken its pace till it came alongside her. The man quickly dismounted, made Molly a sweeping bow, and handed her a sealed envelope. Then, without a word, he sprang into the saddle and, turning his horse's head, galloped back along the road by which he had come, leaving Molly gazing in surprise at the envelope in her hand.

It was all over in a minute. The man and the horse had come and gone. Molly turned the envelope over and over. There was no address on it to say who it was for or where it had come from. Only the word 'Immediate' was printed in the top corner. What ought she to do, she wondered. Should she open it? Was it meant for her? Was it from a friend—or was it another trick of the Pumpkin's? She hesitated, standing still in the middle of the lonely road. Supposing it was a message—something about Jack—something really true. Supposing she didn't open the envelope—what was she to do with it?

This decided the matter; as she couldn't think what to do with it if she didn't open it, she opened it, very cautiously. And this was the letter inside it:

DEAR CHILD,

I know all that has happened. This is to tell you that I have overheard that the Pumpkin has sent out many spies to stop you. One of them is a little old man; a watchmaker he pretends to be. Do not trust him.

Another (and this one is the most dangerous of all) is a certain 'blind' woman who has been

228

A Warning

sent out to meet you on the shores of Lake Desolate. As you value your quest, as you value your poor brother's life, do not trust this 'blind' woman. Have nothing to do with her—do not believe a word she says—but go straight on past the Lake to the Brown Hills beyond. Otherwise, all is at an end for us.

With affectionate remembrance from

OLD NANCY

Molly read the letter through several times, very carefully. Then she folded it up and put it in her satchel.

CHAPTER XVIII

Molly Comes to Lake Desolate

DURING the next two hours, while Molly searched the remainder of the road, and the lonely country that lay between the road and the hills on either side, she kept thinking of the letter. And it worried her. She could not make up her mind whether the letter was genuine or not. At first she thought it really was from Old Nancy, and then, because she had resolved to trust no one, she began to suspect that the man on the horse was another of the Pumpkin's spies and that the letter was faked.

"One part was true," Molly argued to herself. "About the watchmaker . . . but then, the spies would know by now that I have found out about the watchmaker, and *they* would not mind telling me news I already know if they thought it would make the letter seem more genuine. But why should they warn me about this 'blind' woman — unless . . . Oh, I don't know. I wonder if it really *is* from Old

Molly Comes to Lake Desolate

Nancy, after all! I wish I had some means of finding out." And then, after another ten minutes' search: "I believe it really is from Old Nancy—I'm getting too distrustful," she said. "Anyway, I'll wait until I reach Lake Desolate—and then decide."

Molly climbed to the top of one of the hills, and from there caught her first glimpse of the Lake. It was not far away now; but it was actually no more than a glimpse of the water that she got, because of the hills that surrounded it. She descended the hill, searching all the time—for it would not do to pass by any likely spot in her anxiety to reach some other spot, even if the latter did sound a more probable place for the Black Leaf to be growing in.

Although the water had not looked far away, yet it seemed a long time to Molly before she reached Lake Desolate. Climbing round the side of one of the hills, she at length saw the Lake immediately below her.

It was a great stretch of water, silent, dark, and mysterious, around which the hills stood like sentinels. Across the surface of the water strange birds hovered, flapping their wings and uttering weird 'screechings,' as Mrs Jennet had said. Every now and again they would swoop down on the water, or dart across to some trees and rocks on the opposite shore. Molly glanced anxiously around the shores of the Lake, but could not see anything moving, except the birds.

Gradually she made her way down the hillside and stood for a while gazing into the dark, still water. It was well named Lake Desolate, thought Molly, for never had she seen such a deserted, lonely place. As she looked across to the hills beyond, a slight sound made her turn her head. Her heart began to beat rapidly, for coming slowly along the shore of the Lake toward her was a woman dressed in a long, grey cloak. She had a stick in her hand, which she tapped on the ground in front of her, as blind people do.

Molly stood perfectly motionless, so that the blind woman should not hear her move and know that any one was near. The woman came on hesitatingly, tap, tap, tapping with her stick. Molly watched her. The woman passed within a short distance of where Molly was standing—stopped; listened; then moved on.

At that moment one of Molly's feet slipped a little, and the stones on which she was standing moved, and several trickled down and fell with a *plomp* into the water. The woman stopped immediately; while Molly bit her lip at her own carelessness.

"Is any one there?" asked the woman, turning, and facing in the direction whence the sound had come.

Molly did not answer, but looked straight at the woman. And as she looked, a puzzled expression came over Molly's face. Where had she seen the blind woman's face before? She *had* seen it; of this she felt certain, and yet— Then suddenly Molly knew. It was the same face that she had seen in Mrs Jennet's photo album. It was the face of Miss Lydia!

This discovery gave Molly a shock, and sent all her thoughts and plans tumbling helter-skelter over each other. What was she to do now?

Meanwhile, as no reply had been given to her question, the blind woman sighed, and passed on. Molly did not know what to do, or whom to believe. She had never been wrong before in trusting one of her friend's friends; and this certainly looked like the Miss Lydia of whom Mrs Jennet had spoken. But *had* Old Nancy written that letter? If so, she

Knock Three Times!

would, of course, trust her before any one, and obey her instructions.

"I can't find out who wrote the letter, at least, not yet," thought Molly. "But I can find out if she really is Miss Lydia."

Her mind made up, she stepped forward a few paces, and called in a clear voice:

"There *is* some one here. Can I help you?"

The blind woman turned eagerly, and groped her way back toward the voice.

"Oh, I am so glad to hear some one speak again —but who are you? Are you a friend?" asked the woman anxiously. "I am so helpless, you know, and—and——"

"I am willing to be your friend, if— But who are you?" asked Molly. "What is your name?"

"My name is Lydia North," replied the woman. "And I live in a little cottage—up there—somewhere"—she waved her arm vaguely. "On the side of the Giant's Head. . . . Oh, tell me who you are, please!"

"I am a little girl," answered Molly. "And if you are truly Miss Lydia—I am your friend. Tell me what I can do for you."

Molly Comes to Lake Desolate

"Will you lead me back to my home again? I cannot find my way from here, there seem to be hills all round that shut me in. I cannot find the way out and I am afraid of walking into the water; I nearly fell in just now."

"How did you get here, Miss Lydia?" asked Molly. "I was hoping to meet you at your cottage —Mrs Jennet told me about you—told me to call and see you. . . . But I didn't know that you were —blind."

"I wasn't—until the day before yesterday—I think it was the day before yesterday; it seems a long time ago. I am not used to being blind yet, and feel so helpless. I'm so glad you are a friend of good Mrs Jennet's—then I can trust you," said Miss Lydia.

This was something new for Molly to have people doubtful whether she could be trusted; it was generally the other way about. But when she had heard Miss Lydia's story she quite understood. It seemed that Miss Lydia had been away from home for a fortnight, staying with her sister in the City, and had returned home the day before yesterday.

Knock Three Times!

"When I reached my cottage gate," she continued, "I heard something coming behind me—a sort of soft, rolling sound. Then something touched me—and I could not see any more. I found my way into the cottage somehow—I live alone. I kept thinking my sight would come back. But it did not come back. And this morning—I knew it was morning by the cocks crowing and the clock striking—I started out, determined to find my way down to the High Road which runs below the hill, so that I might get help. But I lost my way. Presently I heard some one walking past me, and they offered to set me right for the High Road, but they led me here, and then they laughed and went away. . . ."

"I suppose you knew who it was that touched you and made you blind?" said Molly.

"I didn't see any one," answered Miss Lydia. "But I can guess."

Poor Miss Lydia, another of the Pumpkin's victims! Molly felt very sorry for her helplessness in this deserted place. Molly was fairly certain now that the letter she had received was not from Old Nancy. But why had the spies wished to prevent

Molly Comes to Lake Desolate

her from helping Miss Lydia? She would find out.
If she had not felt sure that this was indeed Miss
Lydia, she would have obeyed the letter and gone
straight on to the Brown Hills.

"I will lead you home, Miss Lydia," she said,
"if you will trust me. Which is the nearest way?"

"Where are we now?" asked Miss Lydia.

"This is Lake Desolate," Molly informed her.

"There are several lakes near here," said Miss
Lydia. "But I thought we were somewhere near
Lake Desolate, because of the birds."

So she told Molly to look for a big hill shaped
like a head, which was somewhere on the west side
of the lake. When Molly saw it, towering up behind
the other hills, she took Miss Lydia by the hand and
led her away from Lake Desolate.

They passed out of the ring of hills around Lake
Desolate, and mounted a hilly path that led toward
the Giant's Head. The country was very beautiful
on this side of the Lake, but Molly had no eyes for
the beauty of the scene at present. She was trying
to puzzle out the meaning of her letter, and the
meaning of Miss Lydia's story. Had the Pumpkin
any special purpose in making Miss Lydia blind—or

237

was it just one of his wicked whims? And why had his spies led Miss Lydia to this Lake, and then tried to prevent Molly from helping her? Surely, if the spies had wished to prevent Molly from helping the blind lady it would have been an easy matter for them to keep Miss Lydia out of the way . . . to have led her to another lake. On the other hand, if they did want her to help Miss Lydia, why had they sent that letter; the chances were that Molly would obey the instructions in the letter. Yes, she certainly might have obeyed them—if she hadn't seen Miss Lydia's photo in Mrs Jennet's album. It was all very puzzling to Molly.

It was rather slow work leading Miss Lydia, as she walked hesitatingly over the rough, uneven ground, but after a time—a long, long time, it seemed to Molly—they reached the Giant's Head, and started to work their way up and round the side of the hill. Molly sighed as she looked back and thought of all the ground she would have to go over again and search—right from here to the Brown Hills in the distance. But she must see Miss Lydia safely home first, and do anything she could to help her. She found herself wondering how all the other searchers

Molly Comes to Lake Desolate

were getting on and whether any of them had finished searching their part of the country yet—or whether any of them were, unknowingly, nearing success.

Rounding the hill, they came in sight of Miss Lydia's cottage. A pretty, creeper-clad cottage, perched on the hillside, it peeped out of its bushy garden down at the road far below. Behind the cottage the Giant's Head rose up against the sky. It was a lovely, lonely spot.

Molly led Miss Lydia to the gate. "This is right, isn't it?" she asked.

Miss Lydia felt the top of the gate. "Yes, this is home," she said. "Thank you . . . my dear. I don't know how to thank you. You'll come in with me, won't you? Oh, don't leave me till I'm indoors."

"I won't leave you till you're indoors," said Molly, genuinely sorry for Miss Lydia in her helpless plight.

She helped Miss Lydia to open her front door, and the two entered the cottage together.

What would Molly's feelings have been had she looked out into the garden a moment later, and seen the crouching figure that rose, and emerged from

Knock Three Times!

behind a clump of bushes as soon as the door was shut? It was an old woman with little darting eyes and a red scarf wound round her head. Creeping along, the old woman pushed her way through a broken fence at the end of the garden, and, darting behind a group of trees close by, began to signal wildly to some one at the bottom of the hill.

CHAPTER XIX

Molly Looks Through Miss Lydia's Window

MOLLY led Miss Lydia into the cottage parlour—a dainty, fresh little room— and brought a chair forward into which Miss Lydia sank gratefully.

"Can I get you anything? Shall I make you some tea?" suggested Molly cheerfully.

There was no answer, and then she saw that Miss Lydia was crying softly to herself.

"Oh, dear! I'm so sorry, Miss Lydia," said Molly, distressed. "Oh, what can I do? Is there anything you'd like me to do?"

"I don't know what to do," said Miss Lydia. "I feel so helpless here alone. If only I could get a message through to my sister in the City, she'd come to me immediately—if she knew. What shall I do? . . . You have been so good to me—it's a shame to bother you with my troubles, though."

Knock Three Times!

Molly sat down on a chair opposite to Miss Lydia, and tried to decide what to do. Molly felt very perplexed and troubled herself. It seemed cruel to leave Miss Lydia here alone in this deserted spot, and yet if she took her with her it would cause so much delay, and time was getting short now.

"Have you no friends near here that I could fetch for you?" asked Molly.

Miss Lydia shook her head. "No one very near. I came to live in this lonely little house away from my friends, so that I could get on with my work. I am an artist—I was an artist," she corrected herself. "I cannot paint pictures now. I cannot watch the sun sink over the hills nor see the stars reflected in the water. What shall I do? What shall I do?" she sobbed bitterly.

"Oh, don't, don't, Miss Lydia!" begged Molly. "Listen. I know what I'll do. Tell me the address of the friends who live nearest here, and I will go and fetch them. I will bring them back myself—and then go on my way. You will not mind being left for a short time, will you?"

"No," said Miss Lydia. "I don't feel I dare

go out again. I will wait here. You are so good
to me. I do hope I am not giving you too much
trouble."

By this time Molly had quite made up her mind
that Miss Lydia was sincere; no doubt of her
sincerity entered Molly's mind until happening to
glance out of the window she saw some one dodge
out of sight behind a bush in the garden—some one
with a red scarf bound round her head.

Molly's knees began to shake. What could this
mean? What was the old woman with the horrible
eyes doing here in Miss Lydia's garden? Was it
a trap? She looked over at Miss Lydia who was
sitting patiently where Molly had placed her. Molly
moved softly toward the window, and stood, hidden
by the window curtain, looking out. In a few seconds
she saw the old woman's hand come round the side
of the bush and make a signal toward the hedge by
the fence. The hedge stirred a bit. So there was
some one else hiding there, thought Molly. She
turned to Miss Lydia. The sight of the blind
woman's gentle face reassured her. No, if this was
a trap, Miss Lydia had nothing to do with it; Molly
felt sure of that. Anyway, she decided that it was

better to tell Miss Lydia what she had just seen in the garden.

Miss Lydia was terribly agitated at first, and cried, and seemed so upset that she made Molly want to cry too.

"But we must be brave, Miss Lydia," said Molly. "Trust me, and do what I tell you, will you?" she urged. "We must help each other all we can. I will help you with my eyes, and you must help me with your ears—listen and tell me what you hear. And you can help me by telling me where to find things and all that."

Miss Lydia calmed down gradually, and promised to aid Molly as much as possible.

Molly's first act was to ascertain that all the windows were locked and the front and back doors bolted. While seeing to these things she discovered that there were two other spies lurking in the back garden. One looked something like the figure of the old watchmaker, only he was dressed differently. The other man she had not seen before. They were both badly concealed among some tall plants and ferns.

"Why are all the spies gathering here together?"

Through Miss Lydia's Window

Molly asked herself. "Do they know I've seen them, I wonder. They don't mean to let me get out of this house. They seem to be watching all round it."

"What can you see? What can you see?" asked Miss Lydia, pleadingly.

Molly told her. "I don't think they can hurt us—so long as we keep indoors. They're only guarding the house to see that I don't get away, until——" Molly broke off; "until the Pumpkin comes," was what she had been going to say, but there was no need to set Miss Lydia trembling afresh.

Molly herself was in such a state of excitement, darting noiselessly from one window to another, comforting Miss Lydia, and telling her what she could see, that there was hardly time to be very frightened.

Miss Lydia divided her attention between the front door and the back, listening anxiously at each in turn. Presently she remembered something, and called quietly to Molly:

"There is a little room at the very top of the house, in the roof, a room I use as a studio," she

245

said. " If you go up you will have a better view of the garden, and will be able to see far outside the garden, over the hedges as well."

" I will go at once and see what I can make out," said Molly. " But I saw no stairs leading up any higher."

" They are in the cupboard on the landing," was Miss Lydia's reply. " I'll wait here by the front door."

Molly dashed upstairs, found the cupboard on the landing, and, opening the door, saw the concealed stairs. She ran up these to the studio. There were four windows in the studio, one on each side of the room. She looked out of each in turn, taking care to keep well back in the room so as to be out of sight. There were splendid views from these windows. She could see clearly now the old woman still crouching behind the bush in the front garden. She could see, too, who was behind the hedge; it was the girl in green who had met them in the Third Green Lane and decoyed them to the old woman.

From the window that looked out on to the back garden she saw the other two spies still hiding there, and a third spy hiding a little farther away from them. Her eyes wandered round the garden, then all at once she gave a gasp as she caught sight of something that made her heart seem to stop beating for a moment, then start to hammer madly at her side.

It was a large Black Leaf, growing in the garden bed, just behind where the two spies were hiding; so that from the lower windows they had hidden it completely from her eyes.

Molly could scarcely believe it for a moment, and looked again to make sure. Yes; it was the Black Leaf at last!

Now she understood the presence of the spies here, and their anxiety to keep her away from the garden, which contained the Leaf they dared not touch. And now she understood the reason why the Pumpkin had made Miss Lydia blind.

What a wonder the Pumpkin was not somewhere near to guard the Leaf, she thought. And even as she thought this, she saw the Pumpkin. He came rolling slowly along the garden path toward the back door.

"Oh, however am I to get the Leaf with the Pumpkin and all his spies around!" thought Molly.

Then she heard Miss Lydia's voice calling up the stairs : "Come quickly! Hush! I can hear that rolling sound again, out in the garden."

Molly ran downstairs.

"Oh, Miss Lydia, Miss Lydia!" she whispered, excitedly. "Do you know why they're all round this house ?—the spies, and the Pumpkin himself— yes, it is he—oh, hush, Miss Lydia! Do you know the reason ? The Black Leaf is growing in your garden! I can see it from your studio window."

Half crying, half laughing, Molly explained rapidly ; while Miss Lydia wrung her hands together and listened intently.

"'Sh!" she interrupted, suddenly. "Listen. I can hear the rolling sound outside the front door now—*and* the back door."

"Not both at once ?" queried Molly.

"Yes, I can. Listen."

"Then—oh, then it must be Jack as well—if there are two Pumpkins," cried Molly tremulously. "But I don't expect he can help us," she went on quietly. "He's under the power of the Pumpkin entirely ; he'll just have to obey orders."

Molly was thinking rapidly. What was she to

248

Through Miss Lydia's Window

do? How could she reach the Leaf before the Pumpkin touched her. Every moment she expected to hear three taps on one of the doors, and see it swing open and the Pumpkin roll in. She made Miss Lydia sit at the top of the stairs, and she herself stood half-way up, ready to run, if necessary. What was she to do? So far the Pumpkin had made no attempt to enter the house, but was content to bide his time outside. Unfortunately Molly did not know which door he was waiting at, nor which of the two Grey Pumpkins outside was the real Pumpkin and which was Jack.

How could she reach the Black Leaf before the Pumpkin or the spies could stop her? Try to reach it she must, yet she knew if she stepped outside she would not stand a moment's chance. On the other hand, she and Miss Lydia might remain shut up in this house for ever so long—perhaps until the thirteen days were up and the Leaf had disappeared; and then the Pumpkin could tap on the door and enter, and they would be powerless to defend themselves. If only something would happen to distract the watchers outside, just for half a minute, that would be time enough—she could reach the Leaf in less time than that. Oh, how tantalizingly near the Leaf seemed—and yet how far away.

Presently Molly asked, " Is there a tree in .your garden that grows anywhere near one of the upstairs windows, Miss Lydia ? I didn't notice when I ran through the rooms."

" There is one at the side of the house," said Miss Lydia. " It can be reached from my bedroom window—the branches tap against the window-pane. Why ? What do you want to know about the tree for ? "

" Wait a moment," said Molly. " I'll just run up and have a look at it first."

While she was upstairs she had another look out of the studio window also. Of course the Leaf was still there—and the two crouching figures among the tall plants. Molly. had thought out her plan by this time, and noticed with satisfaction that evening was rapidly approaching. For, " It must be done in the dusk," she told herself. " Just before the moon comes up."

She went down to Miss Lydia again and sat beside her at the top of the first flight of stairs.

" The tree will do splendidly," whispered Molly.

Through Miss Lydia's Window

Then she told her companion what she had planned to do. "And I want you to help me, if you will, Miss Lydia." She paused. "I'm going to ask you to do a very plucky thing. In half an hour's time I want you to draw the bolts of the back door and walk out into the garden."

Miss Lydia was startled.

"I know it seems a dreadfully hard thing to ask you to do," Molly went on hurriedly. "But I believe it is the only way out of our difficulties. For the sake of every one who has suffered through the Pumpkin, for my sake, for your own sake, will you take the risk, Miss Lydia? In the end, it may be the means of restoring your sight, you know."

They talked in whispers for a while.

"And you don't think it's any good waiting?— in case some help comes?" asked Miss Lydia wistfully.

"Not a bit of good, I'm afraid," said Molly gently. "It's very unlikely that help will come—I think we must rely only on ourselves."

"Then I won't fail you," said Miss Lydia.

They sat there, talking occasionally, until dusk fell. Then Molly went into Miss Lydia's bedroom, and cautiously opened the window and looked out. There appeared to be no one watching this side of the house; if there was any one, it was too dark to see them, and so they would not be able to see her, Molly thought. She had strapped her little pocket satchel firmly across her shoulders, and just inside, where she could easily reach it, was Old Nancy's box of matches.

Fortunately there was a slight breeze blowing, so that any rustling of the trees, unless unusually loud, would not attract attention. Molly got out on to the window sill, and from there climbed as noiselessly as possible into the tree. Molly had had a good deal of experience in tree-climbing now, nevertheless she was trembling as she lowered herself down to the branches nearest the ground; it was not a nice sensation climbing down, when you didn't know what was at the bottom. She waited for a while, and listened, peering out from among the leaves. Nothing stirred in the garden below.

As far as she could make out, she had but to drop to the ground, run round the corner of the house along the path, or across the garden bed, and the Leaf was on the left-hand side, she remembered, close to a big tree, whose outline could be dimly seen.

Molly waited, full of doubts and anxieties. After all, was this a wise plan to try? was it too simple to have any chance of success? What a long time Miss Lydia was. Supposing her courage failed at the last moment—well, who could blame her? It was such an easy thing for Miss Lydia to do, and yet such a hard thing. The Pumpkin was almost sure to catch her—poor Miss Lydia—but it would only be a momentary triumph; Molly would soon see that things were put right again—that is, if the Pumpkin did not catch Molly too. But Molly dared not think about that. She was strung up to such a pitch of nervous excitement that every second seemed like a whole minute, while she waited. How brave it would be of Miss Lydia if she did— But what a long time she was. Could anything have happened to her? Perhaps the Pumpkin had. . . . Hark! what was that!

It was the sound of the back door bolts being withdrawn.

Instantly there was a stir in the garden, and a subdued murmuring floated up to Molly's ears.

Knock Three Times!

The back door was flung open noisily, and footsteps could be heard on the path. Molly got out her box of matches.

The garden was now alive with whispering figures. Several moved quickly toward the back door; there was a scuffle; a scream; the sound of footsteps running, and a dull thud, thud; then the sound of many voices, calling, shouting directions, raised high as if in some dispute.

In the midst of all this Molly dropped to the ground and ran rapidly round the corner of the house, bounded over the garden bed, skirting the clump of plants where she had seen the two spies hiding, and made straight for the big tree. Just as she reached the spot where she thought the Black Leaf was, she felt some one grab hold of her arm and she was jerked back.

"Here she is! Here she is! That's not her at the back door! Here she is! Ah, ha. . . .!" screamed a voice in the darkness beside her, the voice of the old woman with the horrible eyes, who had evidently run to guard the Leaf when the back door opened. "Quick! Come quick! Here she is! *Now* I've got you, my beauty!"

Through Miss Lydia's Window

Immediately there was an uproar. The rush of many feet, shouts, exclamations, came from every direction. There had evidently been far more spies hiding in the garden than Molly had known.

Quick as thought, she struck one of Old Nancy's matches, and as the light spurted out of the darkness, she flashed the flame across the hands that were gripping her arm. With a cry of pain the old woman loosened her grasp, and Molly wriggled and, darting forward, clutched at the stalk of the Black Leaf—and plucked it.

Holding the flaring match in one hand, high above her head, and clasping the Black Leaf firmly in the other hand, Molly called out in a clear voice the words Old Nancy had told her:

"Come to me, Grey Pumpkin! I command you by the Black Leaf!"

Slowly, very slowly, there emerged from the darkness two Grey Pumpkins. As they rolled toward her, Molly glanced hesitatingly from one to the other; then, as they came within reach, she stooped and hastily touched both with the Leaf. The Pumpkins rocked to and fro for a second, then became still at her feet.

Knock Three Times!

The Grey Pumpkin was conquered at last.

Molly stood silent. She could hardly realize that it was true. After a while she became aware of a curious stillness in the garden; the Pumpkin's friends had quietly crept away.

Molly looked down at the Pumpkins in front of her, vaguely disappointed. She had somehow had a feeling that Jack would be restored to her directly she had found the Black Leaf. The two Grey Pumpkins at her feet looked each exactly the same as the other—she could not tell which was the real Grey Pumpkin herself. This, then, was the Pumpkin's object in turning Jack into a likeness of himself; this was his last revenge. Poor Molly, she had been looking forward eagerly to seeing Jack again; there was so much good news to share with him; and so, in her moment of triumph, Molly's eyes were full of tears.

"I can't understand it," she thought. "I expected he would change back when I touched him with the Black Leaf. . . . I must take them both back to Old Nancy; she'll know what to do."

Then, with a pang of remorse, she remembered Miss Lydia.

Through Miss Lydia's Window

"Follow me," said Molly to the Pumpkins, and they obeyed her. It was strange that both of them obeyed the holder of the Black Leaf, but they did, following about a couple of yards behind her.

At the door of the cottage she found Miss Lydia lying on the ground, her face white and her eyes closed. Molly called her by name, but she did not answer. It was growing a little lighter now, as the moon was beginning to appear. Molly groped her way into the house and fetched some water, and knelt and bathed Miss Lydia's forehead, calling her gently from time to time. It was a curious scene in the dim garden. Molly on her knees beside Miss Lydia, the Black Leaf tucked into the strap of her satchel, while on each side of the doorway, like sentinels, were two motionless Grey Pumpkins.

At length Miss Lydia stirred, and gradually recovered. Presently she opened her eyes, then gave a glad cry.

"Oh, I can see! I can see!" she said. "Oh, my dear!" And she cried a little, then began to laugh.

Molly told her quickly what had happened, and Miss Lydia was overjoyed at beholding the Black Leaf in Molly's hand, and the Pumpkin waiting for commands, though she was grieved and puzzled that Molly's brother had not yet been restored. She, herself, could not remember anything after she had come outside into the garden.

"I felt something bump against me, and I fell—and that's all," she said. "But I'm better now."

"The first thing I must do," said Molly, "is to set fire to the nearest beacon. They are marked on my map . . . . there is one being guarded on a hill close by."

Half an hour later a flame sprang out of the night, on the top of a hill near the Giant's Head. Spreading rapidly, the fire darted and leapt, rising higher and higher, until it became a great mass of blazing light.

People far and near stopped and gazed, crying excitedly to each other. "Look! Look! It's the beacon —the first beacon! The Black Leaf is found!"

And as they watched, an answering beacon leapt forth from a neighbouring height. Hill after hill took up the glad news and passed it on, until the beacons, blazing throughout the kingdom, turned night into day.

CHAPTER XX

What Happened Outside Old Nancy's Cottage

MOLLY had struck the last but one of Old Nancy's matches in order to set light to the beacon. And now she and Miss Lydia, and the two men who had been guarding the beacon, stood on the hilltop gazing out at the answering light on the neighbouring hill. The fire cast a red glow over them all, and over the silent Grey Pumpkins in their midst. It could be seen that the guards wore curious dark red boots; these were part of Old Nancy's magic protection against the Pumpkin and his spies, as also was' the white circle chalked on the ground around the fire.

As they gazed down from the hill one of the guards told Molly the quickest way back to the East Gate of the City. If she followed the High Road, which was dimly visible far below, for about a mile she would come to a lane with a sign-post which said, 'To the Orange Wood.' Go to the bottom of this lane, over a little bridge across the river, and then along another lane which skirted the wood, and she would find herself in the village at the edge of the Goblin's Heath. Back over the Heath was the shortest way then. But she would save several miles by going along the High Road at first.

Molly was very pleased to hear of this short cut, as she had not thought of looking up her map yet; and so, being very anxious to reach Old Nancy, Molly and Miss Lydia, who had determined to return with her, said good-bye to the guards and started off down the hillside, followed by the two Pumpkins.

As they went along Molly insisted on Miss Lydia, who looked very tired and exhausted, having two of the little brown square sweets that Old Nancy had given her; and she ate two herself. After a few minutes both she and Miss Lydia felt much refreshed, and fit for the journey in front of them. It was strange and delightful to Molly to know that there was nothing now to be afraid of; no more dodging and hiding and distrusting everybody.

Outside Old Nancy's Cottage

When they neared the bottom of the hill, they caught sight of a figure emerging from a wood on the opposite side of the High Road. The person stood gazing up at the blazing beacon, spellbound; then all at once gave a whoop of joy and did a sort of step-dance in the road.

"Oh!" cried Molly, delighted. "It is—it's Glan!"

And Glan it was, sure enough. He raced to meet them as soon as he saw the little party moving down.

"So it *is* you, little lady. You've done it, after all!" he shouted, as he came toward them. "Well done, well done!" and he seized Molly's hand and shook it till he nearly shook it off. "But where's your brother?" he asked, noting, with puzzled eyes, the two Pumpkins.

Molly told him what had happened to Jack, as they all moved onward to the High Road; and then she went on to explain where she found the Black Leaf, and how bravely Miss Lydia had acted.

"Madam, I'm proud to meet you," said Glan, shaking hands with Miss Lydia. "If I had only known, I could have come to your aid. I was

261

not so far away, finishing searching that wood, which is my boundary; you remember, I mentioned that part of my search-ground joined yours," he turned to Molly, "but, of course, I knew nothing, till I saw that blaze in the sky," he waved his hand toward the beacon. "You're not worrying about your brother, are you, little lady?" he inquired, peering anxiously at Molly. "Don't do that. Old Nancy will soon put things right, I feel sure."

As they went along he told them some of his adventures, and the narrow escapes he had had from being caught by the spies; his 'poor old Father' had been nearly caught once also.

By the time he had finished they were well on the way back along the High Road. It seemed to Molly that the return journey developed into something like a triumphal procession. She would rather have gone back quietly without any fuss, but the people who ran out to meet her seemed so deeply thankful and so full of gratitude that she had not the heart to wish them not to cheer. There were many glances of awe directed at the two Pumpkins as they rolled steadily along side by side. Many of the people followed Molly, and Miss Lydia, and

262

Outside Old Nancy's Cottage

Glan, all the way back to the City—a straggling crowd that grew in numbers, collecting people from every house that was passed on the road. Presently the High Road was left behind and they took the short cut through the lane that went near the Orange Wood.

Here Molly saw Farmer and Mrs Rose hurrying to join them, and she had to explain something of what had happened as they walked on beside her.

They went through the village, and all the people turned out and cheered them in magnificent style, and Miss Marigold and Timothy hastened to join the crowd. It was a strange crowd, made up of all sorts of people, little and big, old and young, that flocked round the little girl and the two Grey Pumpkins that followed close behind her. The people's awe of the Pumpkin was not easily overcome, and they kept a respectful distance in spite of the fact that the little girl held in her hand the Black Leaf.

Out over the Goblin's Heath they all trooped. There were rustlings in the bushes here, and darting little figures that scampered across their path, which made Glan laugh hilariously. From the Goblin's

Knock Three Times!

Heath they could see the beacons blazing on the hills for miles round.

When they entered the Second Green Lane they saw a figure bustling along in front of them, that Molly recognized at once. It was Mr Papingay on his way to the City. He seemed glad to see Molly again, and inquired immediately about his Black Leaf.

" I haven't shown it yet, but I'm going to," said Molly. "I've kept it carefully. Think what all these people will say when they see it—when we reach the City!"

At which he beamed and seemed content. Glan greeted him heartily, slapping him on the back and calling him 'Uncle'; and they walked on together arm in arm, both of them talking unceasingly. Whether either of them listened to a word the other said is more than any one can say.

When they reached the High Road again they could hear all the bells in the City ringing, and people were watching anxiously from the top of the City walls. "Here they are! Here they are!" cried somebody, and then such a cheer went up that the sound of the bells was drowned altogether for a few moments.

Outside Old Nancy's Cottage

To Molly the return journey had seemed very short, partly because of the short cuts they had taken, and partly because they had been able to keep straight ahead, as there was now no searching or dodging to delay them. But altogether they had travelled many miles and had been several hours on the journey, and the night was now far advanced. It was a perfect night, warm and still and clear, for the moon sailed overhead, flooding the land with its beautiful white light.

Many of the citizens had already gone out on to the hill by the West Gate, in readiness to see them pass down to Old Nancy's. Those that were left joined in the procession at the rear. On passing Glan's shop they found that his Father and Aunt Janet had already gone ahead, as they did not know which way the procession was coming, and they wanted 'a front seat,' Glan said.

Outside the West Gate the King was waiting, and he put his hands on Molly's shoulders and thanked her very sincerely in the name of the country. Then he walked with her down the hill, and she told him about Jack.

The hill was packed with people, eager, murmur-

265

ing, straining to catch a glimpse of Molly and the Pumpkins. As she drew near Old Nancy's cottage, Molly saw that a wide space had been cleared around the cottage by the City guards; and there was Old Nancy standing waiting by her door, the firelight flickering in the room behind her, just as she had stood when Molly had last seen her.

She held out her hands to Molly when she caught sight of the little girl. The King gently urged Molly forward, and so she stepped out alone into the open space, and went toward Old Nancy, the two Pumpkins following obediently. Then a strange hush fell over the huge crowd gathered on the hill, and every one waited expectantly for what was about to happen.

"Here is the Black Leaf," said Molly, handing the Leaf to Old Nancy. "And here is the Grey Pumpkin—and Jack."

Old Nancy stooped and kissed Molly on the forehead. "My dear, how can I thank you," she said. "But tell me how this happened," and she motioned toward the two Pumpkins.

Molly explained. The people around could not hear what Molly said, but the whisper ran from one

Outside Old Nancy's Cottage

to the other that one of the Pumpkins was the little girl's brother who was under a spell.

"Oh, will you bring Jack back again?" begged Molly anxiously.

Old Nancy looked gravely at each of the Pumpkins in turn. "Which *is* Jack," she muttered to herself. Then she peered closer—stretching out her hand and turning each of the Pumpkins over and round about. The crowd gasped when she first touched the Pumpkins; it was difficult to get used to the idea that the Pumpkin was harmless now. "A pin was stuck in the Pumpkin pincushion," she said to herself. "Let me see now, let me see now. . . . Ah. . . . Then *this* one is the Grey Pumpkin," cried Old Nancy, triumphantly. "For there is a big pin stuck through the top of him now."

A great cheer went up from the crowd, though those at the back did not know what they were cheering about.

Old Nancy touched the Grey Pumpkin three times with the Black Leaf. The Pumpkin trembled, rocked, then was still.

"The Grey Pumpkin is now completely in my power," said Old Nancy. "But before we punish him

267

let us make sure that he has remedied all the mischief he has done. Most of you who have suffered through him probably found that you were suddenly released from the spells which had held you—as soon as the Black Leaf was plucked. Is that correct?"

Murmurs of assent came from the crowd. Old Nancy asked any who were still suffering from spells put on them by the Pumpkin to step forward; and waited; but no one stepped forward. Molly looked across at Miss Lydia and smiled.

"Then there is only this one last case to restore." Old Nancy pointed to one of the Grey Pumpkins. "This spell was different from the others, because it was worked upon a person from the Impossible World." She hesitated, looking down at the Pumpkin which was supposed to contain Jack.

Molly saw some one signalling wildly to her from the crowd. It was Mr Papingay.

"Don't forget," he called to Molly in a loud aside. "Now's the time!"

Molly remembered her promise, and opening her little satchel rummaged about inside, then took out Mr Papingay's painted black leaf, and unfolded it.

"What is that?" asked Old Nancy.

Outside Old Nancy's Cottage

"It is a black leaf which Mr Papingay painted, and which I promised to show everybody, and he wants me to do it now," said Molly, holding it out.

A flicker of a smile showed at the corners of Old Nancy's mouth, but she sternly repressed it. She took the painted leaf and gazed at it for a moment, then muttered something in an undertone and made a sign across the leaf with her left hand, holding the real Black Leaf and the painted leaf together in her right.

"Have you any of the matches left that I gave you?" she asked Molly.

"One," Molly replied.

"That's just right." Old Nancy held the painted leaf high in the air. "I want you all to see this leaf which has been made and painted by Mr Papingay, and is an exact copy of the Black Leaf. It is a clever piece of work—and useful—as you shall see. Mr Papingay, have I your permission to do anything I like with this?"

"Certainly, ma'am—anything you like," beamed Mr Papingay, swelling with pride at his own and the leaf's importance.

Old Nancy handed the painted leaf back to Molly.

"Place it under that Grey Pumpkin," she said, pointing to Jack's Pumpkin.

When Molly had done this, she was told to strike her one remaining match and set light to the painted leaf. This she did, and stood back as it caught alight, and little tongues of fire and grey puffs of smoke curled round the Pumpkin. Higher the smoke curled, and thicker it became, until the Pumpkin was entirely hidden from view in the centre of a great column of grey smoke. Every one watched—fascinated. Suddenly there was a terrific bang—then the smoke began to thin and drift apart. As it cleared away a figure could be seen standing in the centre of it.

It was Jack, dazed and rubbing his eyes.

"Jack! Jack!" cried Molly, rushing toward him. "Oh, I am so glad! Are you quite all right, Jack? Are you hurt?" She drew him out of the smoke.

"Hullo!" he said, gazing round. "Oh, I say, what's happened?"

He was soon told.

"And do you mean to say that I've been stowed away in an old pumpkin, and been rolling about all over the country?—well, I must have looked an ass!"

said Jack. "But I don't remember anything—only feel as if I've been shut up somewhere and been to sleep." He found his hand seized by one friend after another, and himself congratulated and questioned by the crowd that gathered round him.

"And so it was your leaf that did the trick, Mr Papingay, was it?" said Jack, grasping that gentleman's hand and pumping it up and down. "Well, I'm blessed—you are a marvellous man!"

Which was just what Mr Papingay, his face wreathed in smiles, was thinking about himself.

CHAPTER XXI

The Grey Pumpkin's Fate

AND now, the smoke having entirely disappeared, Old Nancy turned again toward the Grey Pumpkin. She raised the Black Leaf high over her head and, closing her eyes, murmured something to herself; then she opened her eyes and said to Molly:

"I have summoned the Pumpkin's spies, but while we are waiting for them I want you to tell us the story of how you found the Black Leaf."

Molly felt very shy all at once, but she obeyed Old Nancy, and standing on the doorstep, facing the crowd, she told her story as briefly as she could, without leaving out the name of anybody who had helped. One of the councillors was asked by the King to take down her words in a note-book so that they could be afterward read by all those at a distance who could not hear. When Molly came to the part about Miss Lydia she forgot her shyness and grew enthusiastic.

The Grey Pumpkin's Fate

"I could never have got the Black Leaf at the end if it hadn't been for Miss Lydia," she cried. "She was awfully brave. Although she had been made blind by the Pumpkin she walked out into the garden where the Leaf was growing and where the Pumpkin and his spies were waiting—she went out deliberately—to distract them—while I got the Leaf."

"Three cheers for Miss Lydia!" cried some one in the crowd, and the cheers were given heartily, much to Miss Lydia's confusion.

When Molly reached the end of her tale there was a perfect storm of cheering; she stepped down, flushed and excited, and stood talking to Old Nancy for a few minutes, until the cheering gradually died away and in its place a low muttering and groaning arose at the back of the crowd, followed by an outburst of booing and hissing. Molly turned quickly and saw that the crowd had parted, and through the space made a procession of people was wending its way. They were the Pumpkin's spies; some very dejected, with hanging heads; others sullen and defiant. First came the old woman with the scarlet turban and the little darting eyes; next came the girl in green; then several others that Molly had never seen before—though judging by the remarks to be heard on all sides they were no strangers to the other searchers; among those in the rear Molly recognized the old watchmaker, and the man on horseback, who had given her the letter that was supposed to be from Old Nancy. There were about thirty of the spies altogether, and they gathered in a group before Old Nancy, who eyed them sadly.

"Was it you who scattered the grey powder on my window sill, and made me sleep through the sunset hour, and so enabled the Pumpkin to return?" she asked of the old woman who had led the band of spies.

The old woman nodded. "When some one in the Impossible World pierced the Pumpkin with a pin, the power for good which held me was suddenly dispersed, and all the evil magic that I knew rushed into my mind, and I made the grey powder and brought it to you . . . . heh, heh, heh," a chuckle escaped. "And I'm glad I did. We've had a splendid time, ain't we, ducky?" she leered at the girl in green, who nodded sullenly. "And if it

274

The Grey Pumpkin's Fate

hadn't bin for a sort of muddle we made between us in our eagerness to keep that meddlin' gel away "— the old woman gave Molly an ugly glance—" our Grey Pumpkin wouldn't have bin caught and here to-day, that he wouldn't."

"Tell me about the muddle," said Old Nancy, swaying the Black Leaf in her hand gently toward the old woman, who seemed compelled to answer.

"In the first place one of us led her "—she jerked her head in the direction of Miss Lydia—"to the wrong lake by mistake, when she was blind—right into that gel's path instead of out of it, and when we found out what had bin done and went to fetch her away from Lake Desolate, we couldn't find her. So, in case she came back to the Lake (which she did) another of us, thinking to cover up the mistake, wrote a letter making believe it was from you, Old Nancy; and the gel would have believed the letter and obeyed it, and everything would have bin all right for us, only something put it into her head not to believe the letter, and so she led the blind woman home and found the Leaf growing in her garden. But even then she would never have got the Leaf if it hadn't bin for those matches of yours, Old

Nancy; they do burn," and the old woman held out her right hand across the back of which was a deep red scar. "What put it into your head not to believe that letter?" she asked suddenly of Molly.

"I had seen Miss Lydia's photo at a friend's house, and I recognized her as soon as I saw her beside Lake Desolate—and so I trusted her," Molly answered.

"So that's how it was," nodded the old woman. "Of course we sent for the Pumpkin at once as soon as we found you were on your way to the house; but he did not arrive until you were inside, so we thought we'd catch you coming out."

"Are none of you repentant?" asked Old Nancy. "None of you sorry for all the unhappiness you have caused?"

"Repentant! I should think not," the old woman answered. "No, though we're powerless now— we're not repentant. We had the finest time of our lives; that's so, comrades, ain't it?"

The other spies assented without hesitation.

"Then," said Old Nancy, "it would be best to banish you all, together with your leader, the Grey Pumpkin, out of our world into the Impossible

World, where you can do no harm. Is it your wish that I do this?" Old Nancy cried to the crowd.

"Yes, yes. Banish them! Banish them!" the answer came from hundreds of voices; and for a few minutes there was a deafening roar from the people; but as Old Nancy lifted her hand the noise died away and there was silence again.

Old Nancy moved among the spies, touching each with the Black Leaf and muttering some words to herself; they shivered as the Leaf touched them.

"You shall retain your human forms in the Impossible World," said Old Nancy to the spies. "But all the evil magic you have learned you shall forget. You will forget, too, your life in this world; sometimes you will have vague recollections, but you will never be able to find your way back here again, and you will not be able to do any harm to others in the Impossible World. I am allowing you to retain your human forms, because, bad as you have been, you have not been as bad as the Grey Pumpkin. According to your wicked acts in this land, so will your unhappiness be in the Impossible World. *You* will be very unhappy," she ended, pointing to the old woman.

Then muttering some strange words Old Nancy waved the Leaf again, and the spies moved slowly away toward the great tree on the opposite side of the High Road.

"Knock three times," commanded Old Nancy.

And the old woman, with a last defiant toss of the head, knocked three times. The door in the tree swung open, and one after the other the spies passed through, and the door closed after them with a thud.

All this time the Grey Pumpkin had remained motionless in front of the cottage door, and now Old Nancy approached him and, touching him once more with the Black Leaf, said:

"Go! Back to the Impossible World! Not as a pincushion this time, though you shall still retain your hated shape and shall not resume your human form again. You shall become a footstool for people to kick about and rest their feet on—you shall become a hassock! Go! And never, never return."

Slowly the Grey Pumpkin swayed from side to side, then rolled away across the road to the tree. It knocked three times against the tree, the door opened, and the Grey Pumpkin passed out into the Impossible World.

The Grey Pumpkin's Fate

The silence which followed the closing of the door in the tree was broken by a terrible guffaw of laughter from Glan's Father. At once a wild outburst of cheers and laughter and shouting came from the crowd on the hill; cheers for Old Nancy; cheers for the King; cheers for Molly and Jack; cheers for the other searchers; there seemed no end to the cheering, for the people were mad with delight. But through it all Glan's Father laughed on, until the tears rolled down his cheeks and Aunt Janet grew flustered and alarmed. But Glan only stood in front of his Father, his arms akimbo, and laughed too.

"That's right, Father!" he cried. "Go on! Go on! Let him be, Aunt Janet, he's not had a laugh for years and years."

Meanwhile, Jack and Molly were making preparations for returning home through the tree. Molly handed the satchels back to Old Nancy, and although both the children were sorry to leave their friends, they felt that now their work was finished they would like to return home; it was a long time since they had seen Mother and Father. And so they began to say good-bye to the little group of friends around them, including Mrs Jennet, who had arrived with Mr Jennet — so exactly like herself — in time to witness the exit of the Pumpkin.

The King and Old Nancy had been talking apart from the crowd, and now they turned to Jack and Molly.

"Will you accept this?" said the King to Molly, handing her a little box, "as a small token of our thanks and appreciation of the service you have done this country. . . . It seems a very insignificant thing to offer you, but it has an unusual gift attached to it. Whenever you wear it you will be happy and will give happiness to those around you. . . . Do not open the box now, but place it on your table, when you get home, where the pincushion stood; and when the sunshine falls across it—open it; if you open it before, the special gift I mentioned will not be with it."

Molly took the little box and thanked the King sincerely, with sparkling eyes.

To Jack the King said, "I have just heard that you go in for painting, so I am having a special set of painting-brushes made for you, which will help you to do good work — they are rather special

280

brushes;" he and Old Nancy exchanged mysterious smiles. "I want you to accept them as a little memento of your visit, but as they are not quite ready, I shall send them to you to-morrow."

"Thanks awfully, your Majesty, but I don't feel as if I've earned them properly, you know," said Jack. But the King shook him warmly by the hand and said he had done a great deal to help.

And so they bade the King good-bye.

"You will find that your Mother hasn't been anxious about you—I saw to that," said Old Nancy, as they said good-bye to her.

And Glan said, "Come and see us again some day, little lady, you and your brother. Do, won't you? Knock three times on the tree when the moon is full, remember."

"Oh, we'd love to come again some day, wouldn't we, Jack?" said Molly.

"Rather," said Jack.

So, for the third time that night the door in the tree opened in response to the three knocks. And this time a little girl and boy passed through to the Impossible World again.

CHAPTER XXII

The Impossible World Again

WHEN Jack and Molly reached the fence that separated their garden from the wood, Jack was surprised to find his slipper still lying there—the slipper he had lost on the way out.

"Oh, I say, Moll," he said. "Look here—I forgot to give Old Nancy her slipper back, and now I've got three slippers all alike!"

Which was in truth the case. As they crossed the garden they noticed that day was just dawning. They found the back door locked, but Jack scrambled through the scullery window, which was unfastened, and so let Molly in without disturbing anybody. They crept upstairs and managed to get an hour's rest before the breakfast bell rang.

Molly remembered to place her little box on the dressing-table before she went to sleep, and when she woke she saw that the sun was streaming right across it. So she sprang up eagerly and opened the

The Impossible World Again

box. Inside was the most exquisite silver bangle that she had ever seen. Molly was delighted, and she found afterward that it had indeed some special charm about it, for she was always happy when wearing it and those around her seemed the same.

At the breakfast-table Mother and Father seemed to the children to glance at them rather curiously.

"Mother," began Molly, "do you know who gave me this?" and she showed her the silver bracelet.

"Yes," said Mother to Molly's surprise. "I know all about it."

"Why, how did you?" asked Jack.

But "Ah!" was all Mother would say, and she and Father exchanged amused glances.

It was a little puzzling. And even when there arrived by post for Jack a long narrow box containing three paint-brushes, Mother and Father never asked whom they were from, although there was no name inside.

"I suppose there's no need for us to tell you all about our adventure, if you know already?" remarked Jack. "Do you know everything?"

"Everything," replied Mother, smiling.

Of course the grey pumpkin pincushion had

Knock Three Times!

entirely vanished from Molly's dressing-table, and she never set eyes on it again, though she wrote and thanked Aunt Phœbe for her 'useful present.'

Jack and Molly often wonder where the Grey Pumpkin and his spies are. They have never seen any of them yet, though Molly has seen a ticket-collector who reminds her somewhat of the old watchmaker. Both children keep a watchful eye on all shops that sell hassocks, and always glance eagerly round the room when they are invited out to tea anywhere, but so far they have not come across the Grey Pumpkin.